———————— ★ ————————

THE KILLER KNEW
HOW TO USE A KNIFE

I noticed the open desk drawer. On the right side of the desk for anyone sitting behind it. I got up and crossed to the desk. There was a gun in the open drawer. A 9 mm Smith & Wesson automatic.

Then I noticed the blood on the desk chair.

I looked around. The office had a single closet. I went and opened it. He was there.

A young man, not thirty, dark haired and hanging from a wall hook like a side of meat. His dead eyes stared at a corner of the closet. Blood still trickled to the floor where a pool had formed. Alive not twenty minutes ago.

———————— ★ ————————

"Michael Collins carries on the Hammett-Chandler-Macdonald tradition with skill and finesse."
—*Washington Post Book World*

MICHAEL COLLINS

FREAK

WORLDWIDE ®

TORONTO · NEW YORK · LONDON · PARIS
AMSTERDAM · STOCKHOLM · HAMBURG
ATHENS · MILAN · TOKYO · SYDNEY

FREAK

A Worldwide Mystery/June 1990

First published by Dodd, Mead & Company, Inc.

ISBN 0-373-26050-4

Printed in U.S.A.

TO PHYLLIS WESTBERG,
for patience

ONE

FROM NEW YORK CITY to Chatham, New Jersey, the Erie Lackawanna commuter railroad crosses the Passaic River twice within fifteen miles, but no one who didn't know would ever guess that the river at Newark and the river at Chatham were the same river.

At Newark it's a sluggish body of black water under slimy bridge pilings that looks as if it would catch fire if you dropped a match anywhere near it. At Chatham it's a swift little stream running clear over gravel between banks of trees and bushes. At Chatham there are canoes, not scows; houses, not junkyards; ranch-style tracts and two-story Colonials, not tenements or urban-renewal cellblocks.

Only fifteen miles.

I thought about the human time bomb waiting in the vast gulf of those fifteen short miles as my train crossed the river that ran clean over its shallow rocks and swept on into Chatham station. But it was a more private time bomb that had brought me out to Chatham this November morning, and I found a taxi to take me along the main street of the old town that looked like the movie set of a New England village: tall oaks and elms, frame houses, antique shops, discreet real estate offices. Until we passed through a downtown that could have been anywhere from Maine to Montana and turned into a long side street to the Passaic.

The cab stopped at a collection of low buildings on the bank of the river with skylights instead of windows, and a two-story office building with the sign Computer Methods Corporation. In the lobby they sent me to the second floor and a secretarial office between two executive offices. The secretary was a redhead who stared at my missing arm as if it were an insult.

"Dan Fortune to see Ian Campbell."

"You're to go to his home. Five River Lane."

"Do I walk?"

"You don't have a car?"

"Sorry about that."

"Well, wait over there. I'll have to call a taxi."

There was no apology for the change of meeting place. The main drawback to the detective business, aside from a little violence now and then, is that you make your living from people's trouble, and people in trouble tend to forget their manners. Then, maybe it's better to make your living from other people's trouble than from other people.

The same taxi driver took me back through the town and down another long road that ended at a stone bridge over the Passaic where it ran between bare old willows. A chain blocked the bridge, and a bright red Lincoln limousine was parked in front of the chain. Beyond the Lincoln, and the chain, the road continued in a loop through trees and a lawn to a large manor house straight out of eighteenth-century England—as befitted the home of a squire in a village named for William Pitt the Elder, Earl of Chatham.

A man leaned on the parapet of the stone bridge. He didn't move as I paid the taxi driver again and walked out onto the bridge. He spoke straight down to the river.

"Campbell got a visitor."

He was a small man. Short, slender, with soft hands, a narrow head, and a pale face under a broad-brimmed pearl-gray fedora that didn't suit his coloring. His fitted black topcoat was nipped in at the waist, his gray trousers narrowed at the ankle, his shoes were black patent oxfords, and he wore gray spats above the shoes. What I could see of his hair had been slicked with brilliantine. The Roaring Twenties.

"You're waiting to talk to Campbell?" I asked.

"No."

He continued to look at the river that reflected the winter morning sunlight in its shallows, ran dark in its deeper pools. He seemed to watch nothing in particular, only stare at the exact center of the river as if studying the motion of the water.

"Then you must be waiting for Campbell's visitor," I said.

He turned. Despite the narrow head, his face was almost round, the cheekbones wider than his forehead, and as soft as his hands. Thick eyebrows and pale eyes without any particular expression. Youngish, maybe in his late twenties, but seemed older. Whatever he'd been going to say, he didn't. He looked at my empty sleeve and missing arm.

"How'd you lose it?"

There was something about the way he asked, simple and direct, that made me hold back on the gaudy yarns I tell the thrill seekers enjoying the event of a crippled man.

"Fell into the hold of a ship when I was a kid."

"How old of a kid?"

"Seventeen."

He turned back to the river. I had the feeling that I had somehow failed him.

"Not young enough?" I said.

He didn't answer or even move. I didn't interest him anymore, and if something didn't interest him it was as good as not there.

The big black man in a pale blue leisure suit who walked down the circular drive from Campbell's manor house did interest him. Enough to make him look up anyway, if not to say anything.

"Left town," the big black said as he reached the bridge. Tall, broad, and muscular, he had the rolling, flat-footed walk of a trained boxer who had been no butterfly in the ring. The kind of fighter who could hit and be hit, with the bent knuckles, thickened ears, and broken nose to prove it, and his interest in me was even less than the small man's. A single glance that weighed me, measured me, judged me, chewed me, and spit me out as neither threat nor profit to him. With the powder blue leisure suit he wore a dark blue shirt rolled at the collar and open on his chest hair, a gold medallion nested in the hair, a narrow silver comb in his moderate Afro, and rings on every finger.

"Sold out and faded," he said to the small man.

The small man walked to the big red limousine, got into the back seat. The black took the wheel. There was no doubt who was boss. Neither of them looked at me as they drove away.

TWO

FROM THE DOOR of Campbell's house I looked back down through the bare November trees to the bridge and beyond, rang a fourth time.

"Fortune?"

In the doorway he was as tall as the black in the powder blue leisure suit and almost as thin as the small man, but with a dark tan from somewhere other than New Jersey in November. Ivy League handsome: aquiline nose, firm jaw, cool blue eyes, a boyish smile, slightly rumpled black hair without a trace of gray. He had opened the door himself but had to be Ian Campbell.

"Who were they?" I asked.

"Who?"

"The men who were just here."

"There was only one. A Negro. I don't know who he was."

"What did he want?"

"He was asking for my son's wife."

"The missing son?"

"Yes."

"Just the wife? Not your son too?"

"He never mentioned Alan. Fortune, I . . ."

"Did he say why he wanted Alan's wife?"

"No. Damn it, Fortune, I don't give a damn about that man or why he wanted Helen Kay! I didn't like Alan's marriage, I like it less now. I'm hiring you to find Alan, nothing else!"

When he'd finished the tirade, he turned and walked into the house. I followed him along a broad hallway of hanging tapestries, a giant sunken living room off to the right as we passed. There was no one in the living room, and the elegant furniture looked dusty. The dining room to the left was silent, plastic covers on a silver coffee urn and two chafing dishes. I could see the dust in the dining room too.

"You always answer your door yourself?" I asked.

"My housekeeper shops on Wednesday."

He took me into a study at the end of the hall. All books and leather, and it gave me the odd impression that it was a real, working study, but at the same time that it had been bought by the linear foot from some department store catalog. Maybe that wasn't such a contradiction, Campbell the kind of man who really worked in a study, but who would also tell his wife or decorator to buy him a study, make it all leather and books.

"One housekeeper?" I said. "For this house?"

"My wife and I divorced years ago, my older children are long gone. With Alan married and in his own house, I'm alone in the whole damned place and don't need a lot of help. Now can we get to business?"

"Any special reason for not wanting to talk to me at your office?"

"No. Do you always interrogate your clients like this?"

"People with a big problem tend to think of nothing except the problem, forget important details."

"I'm not a man who forgets anything important," he snapped. He sat down behind an ornate inlaid French desk of some period I didn't know. "Would you like to talk about why I hired you?"

"Go ahead." I sat in a leather armchair facing the desk.

He swung slowly back and forth in the desk chair, turned a pencil in his large hands. He had been in a hurry to get to business. Now he didn't seem to want to start. Like a new bride, eager but stalling.

"Your son and his wife are missing," I helped out. "You told me that on the phone. How long have they been missing?"

"Two months. No, a little more. I'm not really sure, not exactly." He put the pencil down, took a deep breath. "All right. Alan is my youngest boy. Last year he was still living here and working in my company. We got along well. Alan's a good, steady kid. No genius, but he does his job when you tell him what to do. He . . ."

"How old is he?"

"Twenty-six, I think. Yes, almost twenty-seven. Does it really matter how old he is, Fortune?"

"If I'm going to find him, I've got to know all about him. I've got to know who I'm looking for."

"I'll tell you all you need to know."

"That doesn't always work," I said, "or he wouldn't have run out on you. Twenty-five was old to still be at home with Dad."

Campbell eyed me both dubiously and suspiciously. He didn't like being told he might not know everything about his son, or might not tell me. I suspected he wasn't used to being told anything much, had the impression he was beginning to wonder if I was what he'd had in mind for the job. He decided to continue his story, but his voice grew cooler by the minute.

"About a year ago, Alan went down to the shore on his vacation. One of those end-of-summer screw-arounds before school starts for college kids, built around some kind of rock music festival. Like most of the kids these days, Alan seems to like girls and other people in gangs. In my day we cut a girl out and took her off on our own. Anyway, Alan was always a quiet kid, even a little shy, especially with the girls. Until he met this Helen Kay down at the shore last year."

"Helen Kay is his wife?"

Campbell nodded, his face worried now. "Helen Kay Murdoch. Alan met her down there in Derry City. Two weeks running around in those bars and no-questions-asked motels, and he married her. Right down there, no one from Chatham, didn't even tell me until it was done."

"Now she's missing with him?"

"They were both gone when I got back from Europe, that's all I know," Campbell said. "Except for this. I found it in their house when I got back."

He handed me a brown leatherette tray with a pad of memo paper in it. One of those desk-set pads kept beside telephones. The top sheet was covered with heavy doodling. A single word, repeated over and over. Underlined, made into block letters, shadowed, boxed, filled in: Freak

... *Freak* ... FREAK ... *FREAK* ... **FREAK** ...

"I'm pretty sure it's Helen Kay's writing," Campbell said. "I found it on the bar down in their recreation room."

"No idea what it means? Or who?"

He shook his head. I read the sheet again. The word had been written nine times.

"She's a lively girl," Campbell said, "and damned good looking. Not the kind of girl I'd have expected Alan to end up with. That's one reason I'm worried. I don't know what he might do to keep from losing her."

"You think he could lose her easily?"

"I think he married her so fast just to keep from losing her," Campbell said. "She's uninhibited, impulsive, totally unpredictable. A tank top and jeans at the country club, a satin slack suit to go for pizza. Does anything that comes to her mind, says anything that pops into her head. Open, crude, willful, spontaneous, selfish. I don't think she ever worried about the next hour, much less tomorrow. Uneducated and maybe dumb, but damned exciting. Nothing at all like Alan."

"And you didn't like the marriage?"

"After two weeks? Hell, no. An uneducated nineteen-year-old from Flagstaff, Arizona? She didn't fit in his life, his career, our family, or Chatham. But I changed my mind. He loved her a lot, she made him happy, he worked harder and better, and all in all the marriage seemed to be good for him. I gave them the house across town near the country club. When you're married you don't want to live with Dad, right? Especially if the old man isn't so old, has some life in him, eh?"

"Did they want to live in Chatham?"

"It's Alan's home. His work is here, his friends are here. Not that he has many friends. Helen Kay is a party girl, and all Alan's social life is here."

"So they lived here about a year?"

Campbell nodded. "They moved into the house last January, spent months furnishing it. They asked everyone to give them something for the house for Christmas. I gave them a whole damned living room suite!"

"Anything special happen during the year?"

"Nothing I know about. Alan seemed a little depressed the last month or so before I went to Europe, but that was all."

"He didn't talk to you about it? Being depressed?"

"No."

"When did you go to Europe? Why?"

"Mostly on business. I left in early August, got back in early October. I'd been gone about a month when I got the phone call from my banker. Alan—"

The woman who appeared in the doorway was tall, slim, in a dark blue robe with a hood, and no more than twenty-plus. A girl with loose brown hair, large eyes, and full, pouting lips.

"Ian! I think my father . . . Oh, I'm sorry!"

Campbell didn't introduce me. "It's all right, Leah. Can it wait?"

"I don't think so."

He went to her and they walked out of the study.

THREE

IAN CAMPBELL was a man who didn't apologize to those he hired. The lord and the tradesmen. It doesn't belong only to a baronial society; it's a personality. Some people insist on their rank and position. I'm not one of them and it hasn't helped me. The arrogant get ahead.

I wanted to get up and walk out of the fake manor. Away from the case, away from Ian Campbell. But I sat. We call it maturity—the ability to do what we don't want to do. And a one-armed man learns patience, does most things in two steps not one. It's made me an unhurried man, careful if not always cautious. With two arms I'd be running all the time, but I don't have two arms so I walk.

Or I sit and think.

About Ian Campbell. In the study there was a large TV set, a videotape machine, a stereo and tape recorder, a word processor, and a minicomputer. Campbell liked to own things.

About the doodles from the missing son's house: Freak...*Freak*...FREAK...

Ian Campbell returned. He looked at his watch.

"My schedule's getting tight. Where was I?"

"Wherever your banker called you."

"Paris, right."

"Alone?" I said. "In Paris?"

"What the hell business is that of yours?"

"A new woman for Dad is one reason sons leave home," I said. "Another is the new woman herself."

"We'll leave my private life out of this."

"I'm not sure we can."

"Try," he said. "I'm hiring you to find my son, not to tell me why he left. Now, my banker told me that Alan wanted to cash some bonds. He had a business opportunity. It didn't amount to a great deal, some fifteen thousand dollars, so—"

"Your bonds?"

"His, but my bank holds his estate in trust and needs my okay. My father fixed it that way. Anyway, I okayed the deal."

I got out my notebook. "What's the name of the banker, and what was the deal? Any names you have."

"Joel Mason, First Chatham Trust. The deal was an interest in a fast-food outlet up in Livingston Mall. Some friends of Alan's are principals, and it should have been a good investment. The only name I heard is Andrew Katz."

"And Alan never made the deal?"

"No."

For the first time I saw what could be fear in his cool blue eyes. He seemed to listen in the big, silent house. Maybe for the sound of his son's footsteps.

"I stayed in Europe another month. It was important for me. How did I know Alan was going to disappear?" Justifying himself before he'd been accused. By anyone but himself.

"You think you could be the reason they left?"

"They went while I was away. How can I help thinking it had something to do with me? At least that if I'd been here I could have talked to Alan."

No one thinks only of themselves except maybe saints and psychos. He'd said he didn't really care why Alan and his wife had left town. He cared, wanted to know why. We all need reasons, explanations. Something to hold onto, the way he held tight to the arms of his desk chair.

"I got home in early October, and they were gone. Lock, stock, and barrel. No note, no calls, no word to anyone. The house sold at a loss! All the furniture! The bond money never invested! Quit his job at the company without an hour's notice! I was furious! I called everywhere. My ex-wife up in Syracuse. Helen Kay's brother in Flagstaff. What few friends Alan had. My other kids. The fast-food place up in Livingston. No one knew anything. I searched their house and his desk at the office. I checked their mail and their telephone bills. No long-distance calls, no special mail. Nothing."

He stared past me toward the open study door as if looking for answers in the baronial shadows of his hallway, maybe for reasons. "Another month passed and then two more weeks. Over two months since anyone had seen or heard from them, and suddenly I began to be worried, even scared. I remembered that doodling I'd found. What did it mean? I decided to call you."

"Why me?"

"Our police chief knows a New York policeman named Pearce. He recommended you."

Captain Pearce was probably glad to get me out of town.

"How much did Alan get for the house?"

"In cash, twenty thousand. A local bank carried the paper, I've bought it back. I lost damned near the twenty thousand on the deal."

"Why buy it back then?"

Campbell shrugged, watched something outside the study windows. A hard-nosed businessman, but we all get sentimental now and then, even generous. The house would be here when Alan and his wife returned.

"Why did Alan need money?" I asked.

"I don't know. I didn't know he did."

"If you figure about five thousand for the furniture, that makes forty thousand. A nice chunk of cash."

Campbell said nothing.

"How much was he paid?" I asked.

"He had a decent salary."

"What's decent?"

"Fifteen thousand a year."

By the current standards it was barely enough to support one young man like Alan, much less a wife who liked to live a little. Campbell knew it.

"He only started in the company two years ago. He was due for a good raise, and if he needed money he only had to ask me."

"Maybe he didn't like having to ask," I said. "He's twenty-six and a married man. Maybe he had to prove to himself and his new wife that he didn't need Dad, that he was worth more than a $15,000 handout from Dad, that he could cut his own path. Maybe he found a better deal than a junior partnership in a fast-food store, needed more cash to swing it, and knew you wouldn't give it to him."

"If he had a real need, a legitimate need, I'd have given it to him."

I shook my head. "I don't think so, Mr. Campbell. Short of life and death, no father would hand out forty thousand dollars. Not without wanting to know what it was all about and probably butting in, even taking over. Maybe he just wanted to be sure it would be all his deal."

Campbell was silent again.

"Or," I said, "maybe his need wasn't so legitimate."

That was too much for him. He jumped up, began to pace the elegant study. "Find them, Fortune. And bring them home."

I stood. "I'll need pictures, the address of the house they sold, who they sold it to, their car make and license, and a retainer. I get three hundred dollars a day plus expenses, for a missing-person job I need at least a week in advance."

"Get your money from my controller at the office."

While he looked up the information, I wondered how he was going to hide me on the company books? He'd find a way. Good businessmen write off everything on the company except maybe alimony. One of the advantages. Campbell found and wrote down the address of the house, the name of the real estate man who had bought it from Alan, the car license and make—1980 BMW sedan. He took two color snapshots from the desk drawer. "Taken down there in Derry City last year."

Alan Campbell and his wife stood in front of the Shamrock Motel. They were in clowning poses, probably drunk as well as young and at the end of summer. Alan was a medium-sized man with lank blond hair and a mustache that drooped below the corners of his mouth in the current fashion. His face was bland, with anxious eyes and a smile of the kind intended to please. A nice, unconfident young man who had inherited little from his father.

Helen Kay Campbell, née Murdoch, was something else.
A small girl, she had large breasts well displayed, a narrow
waist, round hips, and a flat belly. Her face was a lot more
than pretty. Good bones, slightly buck teeth, lips soft even
in a snapshot. A big laugh, open and unrestrained. I could
almost feel the excitement about her Campbell had described. Yet there was something more. She wore her dark
hair almost as short as a man's. There was a fierceness in her
eyes, almost belligerence, that said she'd put up a hell of a
fight if anyone messed with her. Despite the face and figure, more wiry than willowy, a street girl.

Both of them were dressed in jeans and gaudy T-shirts,
were barefoot. The girl was clearly the leader in whatever
they were doing, and somehow there was no impression of
any age difference. Whatever they were doing, I had a pretty
good idea whose scheme it had been.

"I have an appointment," Campbell said. I was taking
too long with the photos. "You'll report to me daily?"

"No," I said. "When I can."

He didn't like that. "I want to know what you're doing,
how close you get to Alan. I want to be told the moment you
locate them, is that clear? Call no one else, and contact me
at once. I'll come to wherever you find them."

I nodded, but he went on watching me to be sure I got the
message straight. I got it all right. There was something he
wasn't telling me. It wasn't just important that he reach his
son; it was important that he reach him first.

FOUR

I ASKED CAMPBELL to drop me off at Alan's house. He
didn't want to. I was already old business, a delegated
problem.

"It's on the other side of town. There's nothing to see, it's as empty as they left it. The buyer never moved in."

"If it's closer, drop me at the buyer's office."

That was better. I wasn't going to take him five minutes out of his way after all, the day was saved. Where he dropped me was a storefront real estate office on Main Street. A brisk man hurried forward as I walked in.

"Yes, sir," he beamed. "How may I help you today?"

There was a time when the used car salesman was our living representative of the breed that stole the West: the cardsharp, the snake-oil salesman, the medicine-show artist who conned our sturdy but greedy forefathers pushing West. Now it's the real estate agent. Look for the dream, you'll find the huckster.

"Mr. Inglesby, please," I said.

He beamed even wider, and I had his card before I could blink. He was my man. I sat down at his desk.

"Dan Fortune," I said. "I'm not a customer, I'm a private investigator hired by Ian Campbell to trace his son Alan. I understand you bought a house from Alan?"

It wasn't easy for him to swallow all that and shift gears from the beaming salesman with a prospect, to a sober citizen being interrogated by a detective. But he handled it smoothly.

"I did. I know a good deal when I see one."

"How good?"

He grinned. "Very good. A steal, I admit it."

"Did Alan Campbell say why he was selling at a steal?"

"Nope, and I didn't ask."

"How'd you pay him?"

"Certified check. I'm a lawyer, so I handled the whole escrow myself. We closed fast and quiet. That's how he wanted it. He had all the papers in the house, signed and sealed."

"How much less did he take?"

"He asked about sixty percent of what he could have if he'd waited for the right buyer."

"That didn't make you wonder?"

"All these rich kids are crazy."

"You mean you figured Dad bought him the house, he needed cash, so made the deal to get quick action."

"About that," he agreed. It didn't bother him at all. Business was business. It was Ian Campbell's problem."

"You never moved in or had the house cleaned?"

"Never set foot in the place after they left. I wasn't in a hurry to sell. Then Campbell came home and took it off my hands. That kind of business I like." He rubbed his hands, a sweet deal.

"Where was your check cashed?"

"I don't know. You want to look at it?"

He went into a back room and returned with the canceled check. It had been cashed in New York at a National City Bank branch in midtown Manhattan. An account number was written on it. I asked to see the escrow papers, checked the endorsement. The signatures matched. I borrowed Inglesby's phone and called the bank in Manhattan. The account had been closed, the address listed was the house in Chatham.

I thanked Inglesby and walked along the busy main street of the town to the First Chatham Trust. Mr. Joel Mason told me that Alan and Helen Kay had taken the fifteen thousand dollars from the bonds by check and in person. The check had cleared a month ago, cashed for deposit in the same midtown branch of National City Bank in Manhattan.

The bank where an account had been opened, the checks cashed, the account closed, and the only address was the house here in Chatham. Alan Campbell and his wife didn't want to be found.

FIVE

THE HOUSE WAS a large Cape Cod cottage on a quiet street away from the river and across the Lackawanna tracks next to a golf course and country club. On a double lot, it was a startling hot pink among chaste white and gray neighbors. The shutters were red and green stripes, and so was the garage door. The grounds looked as if they had never been touched, much less watered, everything dead except a few hardy bare trees.

Campbell had given me the key. The front door opened directly into a corner of the living room, with stairs straight ahead going up to the second floor. The dining room was across the living room to the right, the kitchen off it behind the stairs. A master bedroom was down a hallway to the left of the entrance. Cellar stairs led down from that hallway to a finished basement recreation room with the furnace and a laundry room behind it.

My footsteps echoed in the emptiness. The only furniture in the living room was a cheap bookcase with some torn paperbacks. In the kitchen a solitary enameled table still held an empty beer mug with four dead flies stuck to its bottom. There was nothing in the master bedroom except a telephone with a long, tangled cord, and a man down on his haunches staring at the floor near where the bed had to have been.

I stood behind him. "What is it?"

"A big stain." He didn't turn or look up. "Blood, maybe. Probably two or three months old."

About my height, five feet ten, he was far heavier in the shoulders and chest and outweighed me by forty pounds. Like a onetime football player in a good college, a linebacker or tight end. Not big enough for a down lineman or the pros. In his late forties, a shade fat now, he wore a three-piece charcoal gray suit, a striped blue and white shirt, a regimental tie, and black half boots with tassels. I felt like a pizza deliveryman in my corduroy slacks, tweed jacket, and old duffel coat.

"A lot of blood," he said.

The stain had seeped into the grain of the wood, and the large, irregular outline was clear. I saw no signs of any work to clean it up. The man stood up.

"Police?" I said.

He shook his head. "You?"

"Dan Fortune, private investigator. Ian Campbell hired me to find the boy and his wife."

"Alan's not a boy."

"You're a friend of Alan Campbell's?"

"I hope so," he said. "A private, eh? Ian's more worried than he lets on."

His curly hair was silver at the temples, conservative, but a little ragged, as if he'd forgotten to get his regular haircut. A serious face, handsome enough in a rough way, under thick eyebrows and with a stubborn jaw. When he moved, the athlete was still there despite his weight.

"Ian Campbell's talked to you about Alan's disappearance?"

He nodded. "Steve Norris, vice-president for personnel and security at Computer Methods. I've been looking around, but haven't found anything," he looked down at the ragged stain on the wooden floor, "until now." He looked up and smiled at me. "I won't get in your way."

The smile changed his face, softened the rough lines and the jaw. An uncertain smile, as if he were a man who liked to smile but wasn't sure he should smile.

"I'll take any help I can get as long as you don't want to share the fee."

He laughed. "Strictly an amateur."

I looked down at the stain. "If it is blood, what do you figure it could mean?"

"If it is blood, something happened here." He looked at the stain too. "More than a cut finger. Still, we don't know it's blood or when the stain was made, do we? Could be nothing." He grinned. The grin wasn't the same as the smile. More practiced. A public grin, man to man, and his exit. "Well, I'd better let you work. If I run across anything I'll get in touch."

From the bedroom window I watched him cross the shabby yard to an old dark blue Mercedes convertible two-seater. A classic, and lovingly cared for. He was a man with some values of his own, and he still had that quick, gliding walk of trained muscles. Not ready to play again, but in fair condition for his age. No trouble with the likes of me. But, then, muscles are a lost hope for a one-armed man anyway. For any man, really. There is always someone bigger, stronger, faster, or meaner. That's why weapons were invented.

I returned to the stain on the floor, got out my pocket-knife, scraped up samples of the stain from four different spots. I put the scrapings into a small plastic envelope from the pack I carry in my wallet. Then I went out and up the stairs to the second-floor bedrooms. I could hear dogs barking in the quiet neighborhood, the shouts of children playing, the wail of an infant. Below the upstairs windows the backyard was narrow and as neglected as the front yard. There was no clothesline. Helen Kay Campbell was not a young woman who hung out the wash, if she did any wash. I found nothing in the upstairs rooms.

Down in the basement recreation room a large calico cat eyed me from the Ping-Pong table. When I went closer to talk to it, the cat dashed across the room and out a high, narrow window that was propped open. I wondered if the cat had belonged to my missing couple? Left behind in the rush to vanish? And what kind of people abandon a cat? Or what makes them?

Only the Ping-Pong table was left as furniture in the basement room, but a round light patch on a door showed where a dart board had been, and the walls were plastered with posters of rock and country stars, the rules of electronic games tacked up where the TV would have been, and the covers of road and racing magazines. A built-in wet bar had empty booze bottles littered on and under it. The telephone stood on the bar where Ian Campbell had found the pad with the word *Freak* doodled over and over. The two drawers behind the bar were full of matchbooks and stirrers from various taverns and saloons from the local William Pitt Inn to West Orange in one direction and Morristown in the other. Alan and Helen Kay had stepped out and around.

I found the photograph under a package of bar napkins in the second drawer. A nightclub photo in a green paper cover from the Emerald Grotto in Derry City. It showed Alan and Helen Kay at a table, glasses in hand, obviously high, and leering at the camera. But it was what I saw behind them that made me look closer at the photo. One of those large calendar pads that show the single day, month, and year hung on the wall over the bar. It read: Monday, August 23, and the year wasn't last year; it was this year. Not a year ago, but three months ago. I put the photo into my pocket.

On top of the photo I found a card, the kind doctors and dentists give for appointments. This one had June 17 written in, with no year. The card was from Benjamin De Mott, D.D.S., 14 Winslow Street, Flagstaff, Arizona. I put the card into my pocket too.

SIX

As the taxi drove north to Livingston Mall, I thought about the stain on the bedroom floor. Was it blood? If so, whose? Alan Campbell's? His wife's? Someone else's? Everything pointed to a fast run-out, but were they running to something or away from something? Together or separately? One or both?

"Livingston Mall," the driver said.

We were at the foot of concrete stairs that led up into a mammoth covered mall that looked like an enormous hangar, where they might have berthed the *Hindenburg* before she burned.

"Wait for me."

The indoor mall stretched out of sight ahead, a row of shops on both sides of a central walk divided by plantings, benches, telephones, and stairways down to a lower level. I moved along with the stream of shoppers looking for the fast-food store. I spotted it ahead, walked faster among the crowd, and saw him. Or thought I saw him.

A flash. Quick and gone. An impression...big... black...a powder blue leisure suit...the rolling walk of a flat-footed boxer.... The big black at the bridge over the Passaic, who had asked Ian Campbell about Helen Kay, and had driven away at the wheel of the red Lincoln limousine with the small, pale man in the back. A quick flash and gone into the crowd. Or just an illusion?

Inside the fast-food shop I asked for Andrew Katz. The cashier sent me back to a door marked Employees Only. The manager's office was at the far end of a narrow corridor. No one was in it.

A second half-glass door opened into a large loading and storage area with boxes of supplies piled to the ceiling. There was no sign of anyone in the storage area, and all the doors and the loading-dock gate were locked from the inside.

I went back to the office to wait, have a cigarette, and think about the big black in the powder blue leisure suit I might have seen outside the fast-food store and the small, pale man with him at Ian Campbell's bridge over the Passaic.

I noticed the open desk drawer when I was halfway through the cigarette. On the right side of the desk for anyone sitting behind it. I got up and crossed to the desk. There was a gun in the open drawer. A 9-mm Smith & Wesson automatic.

Then I noticed the blood on the desk chair.

I looked around. The office had a single closet. I went and opened it. He was there.

A young man, not thirty, dark haired and hanging from a wall hook like a side of meat. His dead eyes stared at a corner of the closet. Blood still trickled to the floor where a pool had formed. Alive not twenty minutes ago.

I searched the body as it hung there in the closet. Loose change, a wallet with twenty credit cards and two hundred thirty-five dollars in cash, car keys, and diamond rings on two fingers. The wound was just under the rib cage. A long, thin knife that had angled up into his heart. The killer knew how to use a knife to kill with no sound from his victim.

I called the police, sat down again to wait. After a time the cashier came back and asked where Mr. Katz was. I told him. He stared at the dead man in the closet. It was Andrew Katz.

"I got to call Mr. Margiotta and Mr. Craig," he said. "I mean, Jesus, I got to tell Mr. Craig and Mr. Margiotta. I—"

The police took him off my hands, took Andrew Katz down from the hook, and took my story. They checked with Ian Campbell. He wasn't in his office, but the redheaded secretary confirmed that I was working for him. When the New York police said that I was who I said I was, the Livingston cops got friendlier and asked my advice. The big-city sleuth. They had found nothing missing from the safe, we agreed it didn't look like robbery, and I pointed out the open drawer with the gun in it.

"I think maybe he tried for his gun, the killer stopped him." The only other idea I had was that the killer had been a pro. They didn't like that. In northern New Jersey the police are sensitive about the Mafia. They warned me not to talk about the murder, and let me go.

Outside, the shop was empty now, closed and cordoned off by the police. Two more young men in their thirties sat together at the long, empty counter and looked worried. Worried and scared. I introduced myself, told them why I was there.

"Campbell never came in with us. Just me, Lou, and Andy," the shorter of the two said. "I'm Joe Margiotta. Why would someone want to kill Andy?"

"It gotta be a robbery," the thinner one said. He had to be Lou Craig. I'm a clever detective. "You know Andy. He'd fight. You know that, Joe."

"A fighter," Margiotta said. "No one pushed Andy around."

"Jesus!" Lou said.

I said, "Can you think of any business reason for his murder? Anything personal?"

"Who murders for fried chicken?" Margiotta said.

"Andy's married ten years, they still hold hands," Lou Craig said. "Christ, Joe, who tells Louise?"

"Maybe someone wanted a share of the business," I said. "Maybe of a lot of businesses."

They looked at each other. There was a real question in their eyes. Both of them. Each shook his head.

"You mean the Mob?" Margiotta said. "No one leaned on me."

"Not me," Lou Craig said.

"Andy would've told us," Margiotta said. "He was a fighter."

Not a good enough fighter, but I didn't say it out loud.

"Why didn't Alan Campbell go in with you?"

Craig shrugged. "I don't know. He only talked with Andy."

"Andy told me Campbell said he needed his cash for something else," Margiotta said. "It was no big deal, Campbell was only coming in for fifteen thou."

"You were all old friends of Alan's?"

"Hell no," Lou Craig said. "At the Racquet Club. Some squash, tennis, maybe a drink afterwards. Casual, you know?"

"We only met him maybe a year ago," Margiotta said. "He'd just got married. That wife of his is something."

"Hey," Lou Craig said. "We can't let the cops tell Louise."

"God, Lou, who'd want to kill Andy?" Margiotta said.

"I don't care what the cops say, it got to be a robber."

I said, "Maybe Andy had a more lucrative business on the side."

"You can get the hell out of here!" Margiotta said.

"No way," Craig said. "No damn way, you hear?"

I said, "Why did you ask Campbell to invest money?"

"We didn't," Margiotta said. "He heard what we were doing, asked us if he could come in. Out on the courts one time. When Andy called to tell him okay, Campbell'd changed his mind."

"When was this?"

"Couple of months ago. Just before he left town, I guess."

"You knew he was missing?"

"His father called us, told us to call him if we heard anything from Alan or about him. Only we never did."

I left them sitting there side by side in their empty food shop. They were trying to decide who should tell the dead man's wife before the police did. They weren't getting very far.

SEVEN

THE POLICE HAD sent my cab away long ago, and by the time I got another and it took me back to the offices of Computer Methods Corporation, it was after 1:00 P.M. and Ian Campbell was in his office.

"What are you doing still in Chatham?"

He was shaving inside a small bathroom on the other side of a huge inlaid desk. A clean white shirt hung on his high-backed desk chair, his suit jacket on one of two stiff, caned chairs that faced the desk. There was also a couch, two easy chairs, some low tables, a liquor cabinet, and a trophy case. After all, he was the president of the company.

"Don't tell me you've found him already!"

I told him what I was doing still in Chatham, and what I had found. He stopped shaving.

"Dead? That Katz? How? I mean, why?"

"Because somebody killed him," I said. "You told me Alan was making his business deal with friends."

He continued shaving.

"I told you what Alan told my bank. They aren't friends?"

"They said they met Alan a year ago. Casual games and some drinks at the Racquet Club."

He washed out his razor, came from the bathroom.

"You think they could be part of Alan's disappearance?"

"Not for fried chicken."

He dried his face and neck, splashed on lotion.

"For what?"

"One of them's dead, murdered by what looks like a pro, a hit man in movie vernacular. It could mean that Katz was into something more than chicken, and Alan could have been in it with him."

He began to put on the fresh shirt.

"But Alan never made the deal."

"We only have Andrew Katz's word on that, and he's dead. The other two back up Katz, but they might not know the truth if Alan and Katz were into something special, or they could be lying."

"You're saying only Alan can tell us for sure."

I nodded. He tied a blue-and-red-striped tie, bent down to a mirror on the wall.

"There are two things," I said. "It seems that Alan was the one who suggested the deal, and then pulled out just before he and Helen Kay vanished. It could mean that the whole thing was just so he had something to tell your bank to justify cashing the bonds. Something you'd approve of."

He studied his face in the mirror.

"What's the second thing?"

"I think I saw that big black who came to your house this morning outside the fast-food shop just after Katz was killed. I'm not certain, but I think it was him."

He picked up his jacket, slipped it on slowly.

"But he only wanted Helen Kay."

"Yeh," I said, and I told him about the stain on the floor of Alan's house.

"A stain? I never saw any stain."

"You were looking for leads to where they'd gone, not for evidence," I said. "Steve Norris thinks it could be blood. It could be."

"Steve? How does he know about the stain? About Alan? What was he doing in Alan's house?"

"You didn't tell him you were worried about Alan and his wife? Ask him to look around? Help find Alan?"

"No, damn it! It's my personal business!"

He pulled at the cuffs of his shirt, angrier than seemed called for. Angry at Norris. For butting in unasked, or just for butting in at all? I took out the nightclub picture of Alan and Helen Kay in Derry City just over two months ago.

"I found this in their house too. Did you know they went back to Derry City while you were gone?"

He shook his head, looked at the photo. "Look at those eyes of hers! Like a wild animal. Alan looks drunk. That's what she's done to him. A leering drunk! I'm damned if I know why I want him to come back!"

He threw the photo back at me and stared angrily into the mirror. Then he picked up a brush and began to brush his hair, shaping it carefully, turning his head to see all angles.

"I'll let you know if that stain is blood," I said.

He turned to look at me. Then he buttoned his suit jacket, pulled down his shirt cuffs once more, and walked out.

EIGHT

IN THE ADJOINING secretarial office I called New York to find out how to get from Chatham to Derry City. The answer was that I couldn't. It was back to Newark or New York for a bus or plane, or get over to Elizabeth somehow and catch the bus, or go home to Chelsea, rent a car, and drive south on the Garden State.

I was considering the bleak alternatives when the door of the other executive office across from Campbell's opened.

"Hey, got a minute?"

A bald head with a smiling face that would have been cherubic except for shrewd eyes under heavy eyebrows peered around the door at me. I nodded and went into the office. It was the same size as Campbell's office but without the bathroom, the liquor cabinet, and the luxury. A couch, chairs, rug, but spartan. The bald man waved me to a chair. He was shorter than I, stocky, probably in his early sixties. He wore a plaid sport jacket, light-colored slacks, a bow tie, and a knit sport shirt. His neck oozed over the shirt collar and his hands were soft. He was soft all over, comfortable. He lit a cigarette.

"You're the private eye Ian hired?"

I nodded. "Dan Fortune."

"Any luck?"

"I just started, Mr—?"

"Yeh," he said, his face going somber. I hadn't said anything that solemn or important. He was thinking of his own problems, whatever they were. "I'm Max Aherne. Everyone calls me Turk. Got the name when I was sales manager over at Data Dynamics."

"You work for Ian Campbell?"

"I'm Ian's partner. Executive vice-president and partner."

"Sorry," I said. "He didn't say he had a partner."

"No reason he should, right?"

His hands fluttered in the air as if trying to shape the air into something he wanted to say but couldn't put into words. Words that would show me that there was no reason for Ian Campbell to mention his partner. But there was every reason, and Max Aherne's hands just hung in the office air.

"Ian told you about Alan, Mr. Aherne?" I asked.

"Turk," Aherne said. "Word gets around. We're not a big company. I always liked Alan, a nice kid. Different."

"Different from who?"

"From Ian." He considered a large painting that hung on the wall facing his desk. An abstract painting, oranges and deep blues. An original. "I've got a daughter just a couple of years younger, and Alan worked here, so I got to know him."

"His father works here too. Do you know him?"

Aherne laughed aloud. "You're sharp. I used to think I knew Ian, but the last couple of years I've started to wonder. I'm still working on it, okay? Alan's a lot easier to know. That's why I'm kind of surprised to hear he's run off. Maybe it's the wife. She looked kind of restless."

"Alan never talked about going away? Selling his house, maybe investing in something?"

"Nope. Not to me. Not to anyone at the office I know."

"Does he have friends in the office?"

"I don't think he's got any friends at all except his wife," Aherne said. "Before he got married he sometimes hung around with guys in the design department—that's where he works—but he's a shy kid, especially after his folks divorced."

"When was that?"

"Ten years ago. We'd just started the company, Ian had all his money in it, and we were all working twelve, fifteen hours a day. Edna met a charmer with more money than Ian and a shiny future. Curtis Killian: investment banker, financial consultant, big in politics. Alan was the only kid still at home, and I guess Killian didn't need a kid around, so Ian got him. I don't think Edna's visited in five years, or ever had Alan up to Syracuse."

"And Campbell became a chaser," I said. "I'm pretty sure he wasn't alone in Europe, and this morning he had a young one in his house in a robe. Leah something or other."

"Aherne. Leah Aherne. My daughter." He didn't smile, but he didn't scowl either. Almost expressionless, eyes neutral.

"Was she the one in Europe with Campbell?"

"Probably. It's not new, Fortune. Leah's older than she looks, they've been together for almost a year."

"And you don't much like it?"

"Not especially."

"You talk to Campbell?"

"I've talked. He knows it's not up to me, or to him for that matter. Leah'll do what she has to. She has since she was eighteen. That was seven years ago."

"She's a year younger than Alan?" I said. "Anything ever between them?"

"Not that I know."

"But she's been seeing Ian Campbell about a year," I said, "and Alan got married a year ago."

Aherne fidgeted in his chair, got up. "All right, yes, I've thought about that. Maybe Leah liked Alan, and Alan got married, so Leah took after Ian. Rebound, revenge, whatever. It's not something I want to think about, but I've thought about it."

"And you've thought about Alan and Helen Kay vanishing?" I said. "While Ian and Leah were in Europe."

"My wife's waiting for me." He took a rakish hat with a feather from a hat rack. "I hope you find Alan, Fortune."

"Where does your daughter live, Mr. Aherne?"

"Turk," he said. "In New York, down in SoHo. Number four-ten Mercer, top floor. When she's out here she sometimes stays with a friend in town. Rachel Greene, Fourteen River Street."

He put his hat on, but still stood there in his office. He was ready to go, yet something held him. As if he wanted to say something to me, and didn't know how or maybe even what.

"Too many Campbells in your life?" I said.

He smiled, then stopped smiling. "You know, Ian never showed so much concern over Alan before. I mean, he never really worried what the boy was doing even when he was sixteen, or where he was."

"Alan hadn't sold a house Ian gave him at a loss before," I said. "Or gone off with forty thousand dollars."

"No," he said.

After another moment he walked out.

NINE

I STOPPED IN the controller's office for my money. It was exactly fifteen hundred dollars—a five-day week at three hundred dollars a day and not a penny more. I wanted to ask if that meant I got overtime for Saturday and Sunday, but they'd kept me waiting and it would be pushing 3:00 P.M. by the time I got to the design department, so I let it go.

The design office was on the second floor and it was coffee-and-Danish time. They all stared at me, at my empty sleeve. Word really does travel fast in a small company. One of them offered me a plastic cup of coffee. Another gave me a Danish. I took both. I'd forgotten to eat lunch at Livingston Mall.

"When did any of you notice Alan was missing?"

"End of August," one of them said.

"We noticed he wasn't around much. That's not the same as missing. Not for Alan. The boss's son, you know?"

"He called in sick for a week or so," another said, "then just never came back."

"How about outside the office?"

There were seven of them seated at special desks and slanted drawing boards. Five men and two women without names, only voices. The voice of the large room itself.

"Never saw him outside the office."

"Not the last year anyway."

"We never knew him too well outside."

"Kind of a quiet guy."

"Minds his own business, you mean. Not like the rest of us."

"Listen to who's talking!"

I said, "Some of you knew him outside before this year."

"Sort of off and on, you know? Before he got married. I mean, he went to prep school somewhere and all that, but I knew him around town summers, vacations, like that."

"A movie, some drinks sometimes. He's a loner."

A woman, the youngest, said, "He was awfully serious, not much fun on a date. I know two girls who fought him off on the first date, said no, and he never called again."

"I always figured he just wanted to be like the rest of us slobs, but didn't know how."

That sounded like a pretty good thumbnail sketch of the last son of a man like Ian Campbell.

"He never talked about leaving town? Quitting? Going somewhere special, some definite place or plans?"

They all shook their heads and became a chorus of noes as they drank their coffee and ate their Danish. I finished mine, thanked them, and went out to call another taxi. I knew by now I should have rented a car. Next time.

TEN

RACHEL GREENE lived in one of those big old frame houses converted into apartments you can find in every city and town across America. Anywhere near a metropolitan area or a university where people have come from somewhere else and need a place that reminds them a little of home.

No one answered my ringing, until an unseen voice from a speaker told me that some people had to work, Miss Greene wouldn't be home before five. I was leaving when a battered Porsche drove into the driveway and Leah Aherne got out.

"Rachel gets home at five," she said.

"So everyone tells me. That'll give us time to talk."

"You want to talk to me?"

"That I do."

Leaning into the Porsche her curves were not as slim as I'd thought this morning. Maybe because she was even taller than I'd thought. Without heels, my height, and taller with. Her shoulder-length brown hair was still uncombed, loose and blown by the wind in her sports car, and her delicate face was still boyish. But when she turned from the Porsche with a paper bag in her arms her intense eyes were a lot more relaxed than they had been in Ian Campbell's house. There was a flush to her cheeks, and I guessed that the relaxation came partly from a drink or two.

"Come on inside."

We passed a sour-looking woman who stared at my missing arm. I didn't have to guess the source of the voice that had told me people had to work. In the apartment itself there were two rooms and a kitchen that looked out onto a backyard of bare old oaks and the flowing Passaic River.

She put the bag on the kitchen counter. "There, now I'm even with Rachel. I eat like a horse." She went on in a different voice without turning around. "You're the man I saw with Ian this morning. Is it about Alan?"

"Yes."

"I thought so. Ian won't talk to me about it, but I can see he's worried."

"Was he worried in Europe?"

She left the kitchen and crossed the living room with long strides for a woman wearing high heels. She took a cigarette from a jade box on the coffee table.

"Who told you I was in Europe with Ian?"

"A guess," I said. "And I met your father."

She lit the cigarette. "Ian couldn't have been worried in Europe, he didn't know Alan was gone then."

"Are you worried?"

"Only for Ian. Alan's not important to me."

"What is important to you?"

"My work."

"What work?"

"Painting. Collage. Sculpture. Right now I'm into scene design."

"Theater?"

"Theater, movies, opera, all of it."

"Broadway?"

"Not yet."

I nodded. "Tell me about Ian and Alan. How did they really get along?"

"Like a father and son. How do I know, Mr.—?"

"Dan Fortune. Didn't Ian ever discuss Alan with you?"

"No. Hadn't you better ask Ian all this?"

"I did. Now I'm asking you. I'm trying to get a real picture of Alan and his wife so I'll have a chance of finding them."

"What makes you think it'll be hard?"

"Because Alan doesn't want to be found." I told her about the checks and the closed Manhattan bank account.

She looked at her watch. "I've got to go. You're from New York, aren't you? Ride back with me, we'll talk."

It was the best offer I'd had all day. After her I was finished in Chatham for now, and even a north Jersey highway beats the Lackawanna, but I don't much trust people who drive Porsches on overcrowded highways. It has to be a kind of insanity. At least an arrogance that disregards everyone else in the world but themselves.

"I know," she said. "I don't go for Porsches on parkways myself, but an old boyfriend gave it to me. It guzzles gas and lives in the shop, but the price was right."

She'd read what I was thinking from my face. A woman who didn't miss much that went on around her, and then thought about it. Somehow, she didn't seem the type to be dazzled by Ian Campbell's blend of charm and arrogance, and I had to wonder if there was more to their relationship than either she or Campbell was telling, or maybe than one or the other of them knew? Then, some women have found arrogance a strong attraction since time began.

I squeezed myself into the passenger's seat of the battered old status symbol, and she headed out of Chatham toward Short Hills. She drove easily and well, and by the time we'd gone far enough east on 24 to pick up 78 at Springfield I was feeling more relaxed about the trip.

"Where do we take you in New York?" Leah Aherne asked.

"Chelsea."

"I'm in SoHo. I'll drop you at your door."

She headed south on 78 toward the Jersey Turnpike through the massed early evening traffic, chattered about her scene-design work. This is northern New Jersey, where you can see what *industrial* really means in the black water and smoking air and row after row of factories, mile after mile of grimy houses packed together on gray streets where the trees are as black as the water and air.

"Slums and factories," Leah Aherne said. She was watching me as she drove. "You look like you hate them both."

"Factories create slums. Industry lives on cheap labor and high profits. That's the name of the game no matter where it's played or when. We hide it under plastic comfort in this country, but those are the only two things that really matter to business: cheap labor and high profits."

She laughed. "Don't tell Ian that. Or my father."

She had a nice laugh, loud and honest.

"Campbell already knows, and your father will have to find out by himself," I said. "How long have you been seeing Campbell?"

"You mean how long have we been making it?"

We were on the Turnpike Extension now, heading out across the dumps and marshes and black water of the Jersey Flats.

"Whatever," I said.

"About a year."

"What's the attraction? He's almost as old as your father."

"Maybe that's the attraction. My father in a socially possible form. Maybe I just wanted to see if I could get him."

The dark water of Newark Bay reflected in the fading November evening light. Above the line of the Palisades I saw the twin towers of the World Trade Center.

"You've known the Campbells a long time," I said.

"Not really, our families never socialized. They always lived in Short Hills or Chatham, we lived out toward Morristown or down in Summit. The Campbells never came to our house, my parents were never invited to the Campbells. There just wasn't any real contact between the families."

"That includes Alan?"

She watched a particularly erratic Buick just ahead. "Alan isn't like the other Campbells. After the divorce, after the older kids left home and he was living alone with Ian when he wasn't away in school, Alan used to come to our house. He liked to talk to my mother and father. They're nice, comfortable people, especially Mother."

"How is he different from the other Campbells?"

The Buick darted from the lane to our left, across our lane, and careened into the lane to our right.

"Ian, Edna, the older kids," she said, "they know. They *know*, you see? What is, what ought to be. What's right to do and what isn't. Who they are and where they're going and how everything will be, should be, when they get there. They were born knowing what to do. They never asked any questions at all, not really. They already knew all the answers."

"Alan doesn't know the answers?"

The Buick was gone. "He's a sensitive boy, uncertain and unsure. He always was, I guess he always will be."

"He's not a boy, Leah. He's twenty-six. He's older than you are."

"He's a boy. Shy, lonely, uneasy. He doesn't even know the questions. Or he didn't. Maybe Helen Kay's taught him by now. She's one of the knowers too. One of the doers."

"Was she the kind of woman you'd have expected him to marry?"

"Alan would have married any woman who'd marry him. If she let him love her he'd have been so happy he couldn't have helped marrying her if that's what she wanted."

"Women that important to him?"

She swung the Porsche in a climb with the locked-together traffic and we topped the Palisades. The Verrazano Bridge towered to the south.

"When he finally got a woman, he didn't need or want anything else. You could see that all last year. Ian fumed the whole year about Alan's attitude. No real interest in anything except Helen Kay. Ian said he wasn't getting rich to leave money to someone who didn't care about it."

The Porsche curved down in a long, sweeping curve toward the broad Hudson River and Manhattan across it.

"Is Ian getting rich? Your father too?"

"I don't know about Ian. I guess the company's doing pretty good. My dad does okay, but we'll never be really rich."

"Why not?"

"Because Ian put up the original money, and my dad put up his knowledge and ability. My father made the company go, but the man with the money gets the lion's share, right?"

"Ever since Adam Smith," I said.

We plunged into the white glare of the tunnel under the Hudson, and emerged into the traffic of Canal and Houston. She turned north on Hudson Street to Eighth Avenue and my office/apartment just off the avenue. When I told her to stop, she looked at my chipped door in the windowless brick wall, and up and down the side street of warehouses and storefronts.

"That door," she said, "looks like something I'd be afraid to open. It has to have monsters behind it."

"Only stairs."

"Up," she said, "or down?"

"I happen to have a spacious loft on the third floor. It has all the modern conveniences, even indoor plumbing."

"Next you can get some windows."

"The windows are front and back. New York railroad. You haven't lived in the city long enough, or maybe low enough."

"You can give me instruction."

I could feel the difference in our ages melting away.

"How about over a couple of beers and dinner?"

She looked at me for what seemed like a full minute.

"I don't think I'm going to get a better offer tonight," she said. "Maybe not any night."

ELEVEN

WE STOPPED at the laboratory I use up on Thirty-sixth Street to leave the samples I'd scraped from Alan Campbell's bedroom floor, then went back down to McFeely's on Eleventh Avenue for the beers. One of those new bar and grills that look like refurbished landmarks of the elegant past.

We sat at a large table in the midst of turn-of-the-century splendor and contemplated the magnificent carved-oak bar, the patterned tile floor, the painted glass ceiling, the potted plants, and the wall panels of cut and stained glass. I had a Beck's. So did Leah. It's a beer with a bite.

"How did you lose it?" she said. "In the war?"

"No." I savored the sharp, clean taste of the Beck's. It had been a long day in New Jersey. "It kept me out of the war. Except for some merchant marine time." It was my day to tell the truth about the arm. "I lost it when I was a kid, not half a mile from here. We were looting a Dutchman ship, I fell into a hold. I got the loot out a porthole, was nailed for nothing but trespassing. Mainly because my father had been a New York cop once, and the cops still liked my mother."

"What happened to your father?"

"He ran. I never knew where or why. If my mother knew, she never told me. I held it against him all the time I was shipping out and dropping in and out of colleges. I don't anymore. It takes a lot of pressure inside to make a man run, especially if he's running out on his kids. A long time ago I decided I wished him well wherever he was. Alive or dead."

"You never had children yourself?"

"No." I waved for another Beck's. So did she. "Too footloose. I wouldn't want to hurt them."

"The way you were hurt," she said. The waiter brought our beers. She drank before she spoke again. First things first. "Children are the only human beings totally innocent, and they're hurt, maimed, abused, and killed more than anyone else. That says something about us I have trouble living with."

I was going to like Leah Aherne. That made it even harder to understand her and Ian Campbell.

"Why did you become a detective?" she asked.

"I got tired of shipping out, never learned any other skill or trade. Just a lot of books in my head. With one arm you can't make much of a living with your hands. My father was a cop, I knew Chelsea and the city. So, a private eye. Or maybe I just saw too many movies."

"Not exactly scientific career selection."

"That's your middle-class suburban education," I told her. "Most people don't choose a career, they drift into it. Because a friend works somewhere and it sounds like good money, or an uncle fixes you up, or you get married and all of a sudden have to make a real living. Those who know what they want to do, early or late, are the lucky ones."

"I guess that makes me lucky," Leah said, finishing her beer.

We drove over to Ninth Avenue and down to Twenty-second for dinner at R. J. Scotty's. With more Beck's we shared a bowl of steamed mussels for an appetizer. All I'd had since my breakfast coffee and toast was the coffee and Danish in the design department, so I ordered the Linguine Scotty's. Leah had the sole *piccata*. The mussels were good.

"How did you decide on art?" It was my turn. No one likes someone who talks only about himself.

"I could always draw," she said. "In my family we assumed that the girls would have careers the same as the boys. So off I went to college, art school, private study, the works." She thought about her career as she drank her Beck's, ate a mussel. "The country's in a time of transition, different people are going so many different ways. To Ian and Edna a boy is a boy, a girl a girl, and their futures are entirely different. Yet it's because I'm an artist that Ian's attracted to me. Are we always drawn to what we wouldn't approve of in our own life?"

"That goes back to the other Adam," I said. "How did Ian and your father get together?"

"Dad was sales manager at Data Dynamics, had worked a long time in design, and had an idea for a new line of computer software. Ian was selling space for a computer magazine, had family money, and liked Dad's idea. So they started Computer Methods on Dad's idea and sales ability and Ian's money."

Our dinners came, and two more Beck's. I hadn't had this much beer in a long time, except on a slow train ride to California, but good company makes the beer taste better, part of the intensity of the moment, a double pleasure to both the beer and the woman.

"There's something powerful about Ian," Leah said as she ate. "A force, out to beat everyone. I remember when he was building his house in Chatham. I hated Edna. Ian was so aristocratic. The lord of the manor."

"Before the company was a success."

"Ian's always had money, land, status. It's not money he wants. Something else. I don't think anyone really knows what it is, maybe not even Ian."

"The childhood idol, so you went after him."

She shook her head. "I wouldn't have thought about it if he hadn't started chasing me. I guess I was flattered. Ian can really chase what he wants."

The linguine was good. A nice combination of mussels, squid, and fish on the pasta with a clean, brothlike sauce. Leah seemed to like her *piccata*. We had coffee. The *cappuccino* had too much whipped cream. *Cappuccino* is steamed milk, not whipped cream. Leah stirred hers slowly.

"Is Alan in trouble, Dan?"

"He's gone for some reason. He sold his house at a loss. A house that wasn't really his. He cashed in bonds and didn't use the money for what he said he would. One of the men he said he was going into business with was murdered."

"Is the murder connected to Alan?"

"I don't know yet."

She drank her coffee. "Helen Kay wasn't happy in Chatham, I'm sure of that. Maybe that's all it is. They just left."

"Maybe," I agreed.

"But Ian doesn't think so, does he?"

"He hasn't told me what he thinks. Just to find them."

"Sometimes," she said, drank, "Ian seems almost too worried."

"Maybe it's the money. He wants it back."

She nodded. "Not the money itself, the principle. Alan sold what Ian gave him. Alan quit the company. Alan..."

"Got away," I said, finished for her.

She sort of nodded. As much to herself as to me. I let it go there, and we finished our coffee in silence with our own thoughts. She hesitated when I took the check, then sat back. It was a good sign, but if I started grabbing checks I'd have to raise my rates. This time it would be okay though, I could put it on my expense account to Campbell. She read my mind again.

"Let Ian pay?" She smiled.

"You're part of the case."

She drove me back to my now dark side street.

"Come up," I said.

"Another time, Dan."

I got out. She waved as she drove off. She was too young for me. I told myself that.

TWELVE

THE SCREAMS CAME from the dark backyard below my open rear window. A woman's screams. Anguished.

My loft is on the third floor with the bed in back near the kitchenette, the desk and office in front, the couch and dinner table in between as separation. The back windows overlook the yard of concrete, wooden fences, and two thin city trees that grow out of the concrete itself.

The screams went on. I saw a shapeless shadow bent over on the dark concrete below, screaming and rocking.

The only way into the backyard, except through the first-floor apartment of old Mrs. Jacobs, was down into the cellar and up the old coal stairs.

When I pushed out through the heavy, slanted door of the ancient cellar I saw that it was Mrs. Jacobs herself there on the concrete. Not screaming now, only moaning, crooning low to a small black shape in her arms. There was blood on her worn sweater as she looked up at me, blood on her face where she had held the small shape against her cheek.

"Who would do such a thing, Mr. Fortune? Why? Such a little dog, Miss Beverly. She never barked, remember, Mr. Fortune? Never. Always quiet and well behaved, no trouble to anyone. Who would do such a thing..."

A small, black miniature poodle, its dark fur matted with blood, its legs and back broken, its head hanging down limp in its owner's arms. The pool of blood was on the concrete more than ten feet from the building wall. There was no way the old dog could have fallen that far out.

"Why, Mr. Fortune? Did you see him? On the roof? What kind of person throws a poor little dog off a roof? Did you hear someone, Mr. Fortune? A stranger..."

I looked up toward my windows. My open window. I hadn't opened it when I got home, and I never left it open when I went out. Not in November with the rain anytime. Not in New York. That was asking for trouble. But it was open now.

"She always loved it on the roof. Everyone said they didn't mind. She couldn't go out on the street, not in the city, and I couldn't walk her after dark anymore. She loved the roof. It made her so happy to run, and there was no danger, and she never bothered anyone, and everyone..."

I helped her into her apartment. She wouldn't let me help her bury the small dog. She would call her veterinarian, just to be sure, and tomorrow she would bury Miss Beverly, but tonight she would stay with the dog, hold it for another night. There were only the two of them. She had to say good-bye to Miss Beverly. In the morning she would think about what had to be done. Not tonight.

"I'm very sorry, Mrs. Jacobs," I said.

I left her sitting alone and rocking the dead dog, went up to the roof. There was no way the small dog could have climbed the high parapet—built by some past owner who had used the roof as a playground for his kids—or jumped over it. On the dirty blacktop I found the footprints of a large shoe with narrow toes where someone had stood at the edge of the roof above my windows. The concrete at the top of the parapet was scraped and scarred, and I knew the marks of a hook support when I saw them.

Down in my apartment there was a trace of mud on my windowsill, and the rug beneath the open window was a hair out of line, as if it had slid a little under the feet of someone who swung in through the window. The lamp on my desk could have been moved. Some of the papers in my top desk drawer seemed slightly out of order. All the desk drawers were disarranged. Not much, but enough.

Someone had come down from the roof using climbing equipment, opened my window, and searched my apartment/office. Carefully and thoroughly. Someone who had thrown a small old poodle off the roof to its death.

THIRTEEN

WHEN YOU HAVE one arm you rent a car with an automatic transmission on the wheel post and learn to steer with your knees. I learned the trick from a salesman who picked me up when I was hitchhiking through Ohio years ago.

South and west of Woodbridge I reached the Garden State Parkway and settled down for the long, easy drive south along the landscaped parkway that stretched ahead rising and falling through the low hills. New Jersey is still both one of the ugliest and one of the most beautiful of states, depending on where you look. The most populated and most deserted, most industrial and most barren.

After Toms River the countryside widened in the flat sweep of the pine barrens and the salt marshes behind the long barrier beaches. The cool, clear morning grew cloudy to the east, and a wind began to blow from the sea. By the time I crossed the Atlantic City Expressway and drove on through Pleasantville to the Derry City turnoff the sun was gone and the sea was a dull gray.

A ring of factories rises out of the marshes on the out-
skirts of Derry City, then the rows of homemade houses of
the older immigrants, the tenements, the urban-renewal
projects already turning into slums, and finally the tall
buildings of downtown. Spread along the beaches and the
shore drive were the office buildings, the hotels, the domes
of the two convention centers, the neon of the amusement
parks and bars and movie palaces. Not the glitter of gambling casinos yet, but that would come soon enough.

The Shamrock Motel was on the outer rim of downtown.
On a weekday in November, the sky darkening to the east
and the wind blowing up cold from the sea along the empty
streets, its vacancy sign was on. Inside, the office was larger
than I'd expected for a motel out of the main streets. It was
furnished with rattan chairs and couches, a color TV, a
black-and-white TV, a Ping-Pong table, a table for games
from chess to Monopoly, two bookcases full of dog-eared
paperbacks, Coke and coffee machines, and a sandwich
machine.

"Looks like a college dormitory game room," I said to
the woman behind the registration desk.

"That's the idea," she said. "We got to compete with the
hotels and big motels downtown. People stay a week or
more in this town, mostly kids out this far. You got to be
more than cheap, you got to make them feel at home. A lot
of our kids come back every year."

She was a motherly-looking type in a housedress and a
sweater, but her eyes were restless, and her arms were
crossed on her breasts as if she were cold. I had the feeling
she was a woman who had come from a lot of other places,
and ended here, perpetually cold from September to April,
with a business barely able to keep her alive.

"Are Alan Campbell and Helen Kay regulars?"

"Surely are. Came back again last August. Anniversary time. Old married folks now, but still just a pair of wild kids."

"How long did they stay?"

"A weekend, on the town the whole time. Only time I saw 'em was headin' out for breakfast over to the Silver Spoon." She nodded toward the front windows behind me. A large, gaudy, silver and blue diner stood across the street, red neon glowing around its entire roof line even before lunchtime.

"How long were they here the first time a year ago?"

"Two weeks. Of course, they weren't together the first week. Helen Kay was here with two other girls. It was Labor Day week, you know. We always get gangs of college kids down here for Labor Day week. Last fling before they go back to school."

She sounded as if she remembered some last flings of her own. Other times in other towns. Before she faced reality and ended up running a cheap motel in New Jersey and watching the kids have the flings.

"Alan showed up the second week?"

"Earlier, but came to stay the second week. Three of 'em. Boys I mean. When the college kids come to town it's one long party. On the beaches, at the rock concerts, in the rooms. Those three girls must have had twenty different boys around that first week. By the second week they all paired off, and the three boys moved in here. Oh, they all pretended the boys had a separate room, but, hell, we knew. They kept it discreet, so we didn't make any trouble."

"What were they like back then? Alan and Helen Kay?"

"I always liked them." She smiled. "That Helen Kay was a wild one, still is. We already knew her, she'd been down before. She was younger than most of them, and the crazier something was, the better. We were kind of surprised she went so much for Alan, but we liked him a lot too. He was older than most, kind of shy. You could see he hadn't been around girls much. But we stood up for 'em, I was matron of honor, and here it is a year later and they're still together and happy as they was a year ago. Just no figurin' people.''

"No," I said. "While they were here this August, did they talk about their plans? About going away somewhere?''

She shook her head, and seemed to look me over for the first time. "You're looking for them, aren't you? Are they in trouble?''

"Was there anything about them this August that made you think they could be in trouble?''

"No," she said. "Happy as a pair of kids with a box of new candy. You police?''

"Private." I told her who I was. "Alan's father hired me to find them. You're sure they gave you no clues about their future?''

"Not to me," she said. "There's Darlene. She was one of the three girls that Labor Day week a year ago. She stayed, works over at the Silver Spoon now. Darlene Winfield.''

At the diner they said they had no Darlene Winfield. I told them the landlady at the Shamrock said they did. They couldn't help that. I asked them if maybe they had another Darlene? They had a Darlene Albano. I said that was lucky, could I maybe talk to her? They said it was okay with them. I thanked them, asked if I could talk to her now? They said Darlene wouldn't be in until around 5:00 P.M. I said that was fine, did they happen to have her home address? They gave it to me. I thanked them again.

I drove along the shore drive as the dark clouds continued to build out at sea. The afternoon light was a steel color now, and the winter sea was a dark green breaking ponderous on the deserted beaches. In all resort cities there is a glittering center where the tourists, conventioneers, and vacationers come, the affluent strangers. Around this center are the smaller, darker streets where the bellboys and waiters, cooks and shopkeepers, taxi drivers and street cleaners live. All the faceless thousands who do the work to produce the glitter of the center for the affluent strangers. The real city out on the edge of the neon.

Darlene Albano's rooming house was on a narrow, sandy street where an inlet through the barrier beach joined the sea to the bay behind and created a peninsula with water on three sides. She had the upstairs rear. She wasn't in her room. The landlord suggested I look out on the beach. She was always taking walks on the beach. Every damned day she took another walk on the lousy beach. Why the hell did she rent a room if she was going to live on the goddamn beach? I had no answer for the landlord. Not a polite one.

FOURTEEN

I SAW HER in the distance against the low black clouds and the sweep of the surf. She was near the inlet, seated alone on the skeletal pilings of what had been a pier, or some kind of bulkhead to hold in the sand. I had to bend into the wind on the open beach, but it was fresh air after the landlord. The heavy winter sand weighed my feet down. She watched me all the way across the sand.

"Miss Albano? Or is it Winfield?"

"Whichever," she said. "Do I know you?"

"I'm trying to locate Alan and Helen Kay Campbell." I showed my credentials. "The lady at the Shamrock sent me to the diner, they sent me to your rooming house, your landlord sent me here."

She looked out toward the ponderous sea. "He thinks I'm nuts, walking on the beach all the time. I'm immoral to walk on the beach instead of hiding in four walls, un-American."

"There's always someone like that," I said. "Did you see Alan and Helen Kay when they were here in August?"

"I saw them." She looked at me. "Once. In a bar. Drunk, them and me. They never came near the diner or my room."

She looked back out to sea, where the surf blew spume on the wind, and then along the windswept beach under the black sky. A short girl, too heavy even without the thick corduroy jeans and bulky gray sweater under a dark blue navy pea jacket. She had a young, fresh face, but tired, with an almost feverish glitter in the eyes, as if she were living on something inside no one could see.

"Did they say where they were going?"

"New York maybe, and maybe Flagstaff."

"Maybe?"

"They were drunk, just talked about taking to the road, moving on. Talked about maybe visiting her brother."

"Tell me about that Labor Day last year? How did you all meet?"

"Sarah—that was the other girl, Sarah Borden—and I were at Rutgers. She was a senior in theater arts, I was just a soph taking some theater courses. Sarah came from out in Flagstaff, knew Helen Kay before she dropped out of high school out there. So Helen Kay asked Sarah to come down here Labor Day week. Sarah brought me along." She searched her jacket, its collar up against the still rising wind. She found a cigarette, lit it, and smoked as she watched the pounding of the surf. "We got a room at the Shamrock and cruised around picking up all kinds of guys. Helen Kay could pick up anyone. There's something about her that grabs men. We were all in and out of the bars, the concerts, and the parties all week. Guys would latch on, and split, and show again, and somewhere along the line we picked up Alan Campbell. He was pretty lame at partying, but hung in there. Sarah picked up a Cornell snob and I'd found

Sammy Albano. Helen Kay was still playing them all against each other. She's good at getting the men to fight over her."

"She likes men to fight over her?"

"She did last year. Maybe she's changed, though. Alan didn't act so jealous this time down the way he did last year."

"Sometimes marriage can change things," I said.

The heavy clouds covered the whole sky now, except for a tiny patch of far distant blue low to the west where some shafts of sunlight touched down like the legs of a giant spider. Darlene Albano smoked and watched the surf break on the long beach.

"You could see Alan'd been spoiled by his rich old man, and controlled too. He wanted to be like his father, but he wasn't and never would be. Nervous and real tense. Only Helen Kay made him relax, brought him out, made him laugh and party it up."

I watched the last patch of blue vanish somewhere over Maryland, watched the waves breaking farther out and sweeping high up the long beach on the storm wind. Darlene Albano was answering my questions, and answering some other questions too. Maybe the questions that brought her out of her solitary room to the open beach day after day.

"Helen Kay told me she really liked Alan. He was nothing like the other college boys or the boys back in Flagstaff. He had brains and manners and treated her like she was special. She kept saying he was so nice, real nice, as if she'd never known a guy could be nice." She dropped her cigarette into the sand and lit another, the match cupped in her hand against the wind. "I guess Helen Kay'd never met a quiet guy like Alan who talked all the time about serious things, and knew a lot, and still liked to have a good time. Sarah told me Helen Kay'd had a pretty bad growing up out there in Arizona. Her parents died when she was real young, and her brother was sick, and they both lived around with relatives and foster parents, and ran around out of school half the time. Anyway, I guess Alan looked a lot different, and she liked that, and it didn't hurt that his old man had a lot of money and owned a whole company.''

She went on smoking where she sat on the weathered piling. She seemed to be back there on that Labor Day week a year ago, reliving it, and not for me or Alan or Helen Kay, but for herself. Remembering how it had been. Remembering herself.

''So the three guys moved in with us the end of the first week. Sarah's Cornell snob, my Sammy, and Alan. We had a hell of a good time the next week. Best time I ever had. Then Sarah got tired of the Cornell creep and went home. The rest of us stayed on a couple of more days, and then Alan and Helen Kay said, 'Hey, let's get married!' Sammy and me said, 'Why not?' and so we did. We got the motel owners to be witnesses, got married in one of the local chapels. Alan and Helen Kay went home to Chatham, and me and Sammy stayed here.''

''Why?'' I said. ''I mean, why did you stay here?''

She shrugged. ''My Sammy was a local, not college. Worked putting on roofs with his father. Twenty-one, no bank account, so we set up house in his folks' spare room. It wasn't so bad for a while, we had a lot of fun the first couple of months.''

''What happened to Rutgers?''

''I dropped out. My parents cried a lot, but I was in love. I was grown up, right? A married woman.'' She smiled but she didn't laugh in the sea wind. It was a joke, but it wasn't that funny. ''Sammy told me he wanted out after three months. What else could he do? I was twenty and couldn't earn a dime. He was twenty-one and didn't even have a trade except working for his old man. He was scared every night I'd get pregnant, and after a while I got scared of that too. Winter down here is pretty grim, we got to hate each other, so we split. His folks were happy as clams, sent him off somewhere fast. I was glad to get away from him and them, kick my heels, find a new guy.''

The wind was a gale now, blowing sand all around us. I shut my eyes as a gust whipped stronger. When I opened them again she hadn't moved on her solitary piling. Like a still photograph in black and white against the gray day.

''The second guy split fast, and I'd had enough. I knew I had to get a job on my own. Waitress in that diner was the best I could do.'' She sat rigid on the dark, rotted piling, not even smoking. ''So now I wait table six days a week, seven if I want some extra cash. I live alone and walk on the beach. I like the open beach. All the space, the distance, you know?'' She looked far out to sea, across the longest distance. ''When I was a kid I had all kinds of big plans. I was going to be a great actress, or a famous singer, or a big-time lawyer, or even a ballplayer. I was going to be *someone*, you know? In college I was trying theater, and law, and even business. I've got a head for figures. If I never did any of those at least I could teach. Now I'm a waitress in a diner. A waitress is no one. A waitress is going nowhere. A waitress is going to do nothing except maybe get married, and what kind of man do you meet in a diner? Some guy who won't even get you out of the diner, probably live on what you make. Losers. And losers stay losers. A waitress stays a waitress.''

''So?''

She lit another cigarette, tossed the burning match into the wind. It blew away across the sand in a brief fire.

''So I'm going home. Swallow it all and go home. I'm going back to college.''

She got down from the piling as if she were going to leave on the dead run for wherever home was. But she only wrapped her jacket closer around herself in the gale wind

and watched a powerboat fight its way through the surging
inlet toward the calm of the bay behind the barrier beach.

"Why are you trying to find Helen Kay and Alan?"

I told her. She hunched inside the jacket. "The only thing
they talked much about was going up to New York and
having a ball. It didn't sound like a plan, just a fling. Some
fun."

"Anywhere in particular in New York?"

"No, but if they went up there for any time they'd probably check in with Sarah."

"The other girl last year? You have her address?"

"I think so."

When we left the beach there were only the sea gulls still
there, standing on the sand as far as I could see in both
directions. Motionless gulls, waiting for the storm to end,
the wind to drop. They looked as if they would wait there
forever. In her room Darlene Albano couldn't find Sarah
Borden's address.

"I must have lost it. Maybe Mrs. Schott has it. The landlady at the Shamrock."

We drove downtown. The landlord watched us leave as if
he'd always known that a girl who walked on the beach
every day would end up with an overage one-armed man for
a boyfriend. Mrs. Schott wasn't at the registration desk of
the Shamrock. No one was.

"I'll wait," I said. "You go on."

"I guess I'll go to a movie then. What a waitress does on
her afternoon off."

"Go home," I said. "Don't wait."

"Don't worry. I know now."

I watched her walk away along the gray street on the edge
of the glitter of downtown Derry City. I hoped she knew.
She seemed like someone worth saving from a long life of
slow regret.

I waited another five minutes, but no one appeared at the registration desk. I went into the empty office behind the desk. A leather address book lay on the desk next to the telephone. I turned it around and opened it to B. Sarah Borden was listed as living at 517 Perry Street in New York. I closed the address book, looked for something to write the number on.

The big hand held me by the neck.

From behind. A hand with fingers almost large enough to circle my neck, paralyzing. The jab of a pistol barrel against my spine.

"Walk."

The hand on my neck guided me to the open door of a small bathroom. The gun barrel pushed me through the door.

"Freeze."

I stopped inside the bathroom. The hand released my neck. I didn't turn. The fist slammed into my back over the kidneys, dropped me to my knees, to my side on the floor. The massive pain blinded me. Waves of black pain, red pain, green pain.

Vaguely, irrelevant through the pain, I heard the key turn in the door lock.

The nausea came. Crawling, I hung my head into the toilet bowl.

FIFTEEN

SOME TIME LATER, the pain only a savage throbbing through the nausea and the odor of vomit, I sat against the cold, hard porcelain of the toilet and heard the voices somewhere beyond the locked door.

"I told you I don't know where she is!"

"I been to Chatham, old lady. You think hard now."

"I want you to leave this office!"

"Hey, Mother, be nice."

The voices of the landlady, Mrs. Schott, and a man. The heavy voice of a man who could be the one who'd put me into the bathroom, but I couldn't be sure. Yet there was something familiar about the man's voice.

"Put that down," the landlady's voice said beyond the door. *"I'm afraid of guns."*

"You supposed to be, Mother."

"I'm calling my husband!"

The sound of a hand, a fist, hitting flesh carried through the locked door. The cry of pain. The fall to the floor.

"Now I'm gonna take me a look around, you got that, old woman?"

"You . . . animal."

Drawers slid and papers rustled. Heavy feet walked. Objects fell to the floor. Something smashed. Something more smashed.

"Harry! Help! Harry! Help! Help!"

A drawer hit the floor, splintered. I watched the locked door of my bathroom. I wanted to yell: No! No!

"Police! Police! Help! Police! Po—"

The muffled scream was like the faint shriek of a mouse in the jaws of a cat. If I broke through the door would I help? Or hurt? Alarm the man? Unarmed, would I save us both? One of us? Neither? If I did nothing, would no one be hurt? If I sat on the floor with my back against the toilet and did nothing.

Silent sounds. Thrashing. Choking. A cry that never came but vibrated under the surface of the silence. The sound of something large, limp, and soft dropping to the floor beyond the door.

I sat against the cold porcelain. There were no more sounds except the unhurried footsteps of the man as he walked around the office beyond the bathroom door. I became aware of the pain in my back again. The dull, nauseating throb of my kidneys. The pain and the silence except for the slow footsteps walking. Around the office. Around and around.

After a long time, what seemed like a long time, the pain deep in my back, the footsteps faded away toward the registration desk, toward the outside door. A car door slammed. A motor started, throbbed, and was gone.

I stood up and listened at the locked door of my dark bathroom. I heard nothing. I listened for five minutes. Then I broke the door open.

The landlady, Mrs. Schott, lay in the debris of the ransacked office. Two lamps lay broken. Drawers were on the floor. Papers were strewn. She was sprawled behind the desk in the same gray sweater and housedress I'd seen earlier. A bloody sweater ripped under her left breast. There was no need for me to check to be sure she was dead. The same small, bloody wound I'd seen on the fast-food owner, Andrew Katz, up in Livingston Mall. A single sharp, narrow knife wound up into her heart.

I called the police, then went through the litter of the motel office. If there had been any leads to where Alan or Helen Kay Campbell were now the killer had taken them with him. He'd been thorough and efficient, just as he was with a knife, and if he'd left any clues to his identity or purpose I didn't find them.

I sat down behind the office desk, lit a cigarette. The voice of the unseen man had been familiar, but not familiar enough to place by the voice alone. Now I had the killing, the knife. I thought about the big black in the leisure suit at the stone bridge over the Passaic yesterday. The one I thought I saw vanish into the crowd of shoppers outside the fast-food shop in Livingston Mall. Where Andrew Katz had died from a single, efficient thrust of a narrow knife.

I thought about that, and about the dead woman on the floor. Could I have saved her? Would I have scared him off if I'd broken out? No, not this killer. Not a one-armed man. Yet, you never knew. Maybe the noise would have been that one extra risk that made him leave without killing. It was more likely he would have killed us both, but you never knew. I could have tried.

The Derry City police were led by a stocky, balding man with a soft voice and a nice smile.

"You the guy that called?"

"Dan Fortune." I showed my credentials. "From New York."

"Lieutenant DeVasto." He returned to his men. "Jack, go find Harry Schott. Break it to him easy, okay? The rest of you spread out and look for witnesses, one guy coming or going, and get the lab teams started on the body and the office. I want the full treatment." He turned to me. "Okay, Dan, tell me all about this."

I told him. The story, and what had happened in the motel office. As I talked he looked toward the broken bathroom door, at the litter, and at the dead woman where the assistant medical examiner worked over her.

"Doc," DeVasto said, "take a look at Fortune's back."

I took off my jacket, pulled up my shirt. The doctor examined my back, felt the spot. I winced as the dull throb of pain turned to a sharp stab at each touch.

"Hell of a kidney punch. It's going to be a beautiful bruise, but doesn't feel like anything's broken or ruptured."

"Thanks, Doc," DeVasto said.

I tucked my shirt back in, put on my jacket. DeVasto watched.

"No gun?"

"No," I said.

"You think the same guy that hit you killed her?"

"I can't say for sure. I didn't see the guy who hit me, and I didn't see the killer. The voices sounded similar, but he said only two words to me. In the bathroom I was out of it with the pain for at least five minutes."

"Yeah," DeVasto said. "You think the same guy killed that fellow up in Livingston?"

"How many trained killers can be looking for Alan and Helen Kay Campbell at the same time?"

"Maybe an organization."

"Maybe," I said. "And so far I'm batting a thousand in not stopping them."

"No way you could have stopped this," DeVasto said.

"I could have tried."

"You'd be dead with her."

"I might have scared him off."

"With what? Your teeth?"

"You never know. He might have decided to leave."

"Because of a guy with one arm and no weapon? A guy he'd locked in the john himself?"

"If the killer was the same man," I said. "They could have been different men."

"If you'd have tried to stop him you'd be as dead as she is. You wouldn't have saved her and gotten killed yourself. This way, you've got a chance to help get him later. There's not a damn thing you could have done."

I shrugged, looked silently to where the medical examiner's men were putting Mrs. Schott into a body bag. DeVasto looked at me.

"Any hints this Alan Campbell or his wife are mixed up with the Mob? Organized crime? Into anything big like drugs, maybe gambling?"

"Nothing solid," I said. "Just that they gathered up some cash and vanished. They must have needed that cash for something. Or just wanted it for something."

"Maybe nothing more than two kids needing to be on their own?"

"That's possible," I said.

DeVasto said, "Except a killer's looking for them. Or for one of them."

We both thought about that as the medical examiner's team carried the body bag to the door. A tall, bent man with a face grayer than his hair stopped them. A detective stood behind him. The man motioned to the medical examiner's men to put the bag down. DeVasto stepped toward him.

"Harry—"

The man said, "Open it. Open the bag."

"Harry," DeVasto said. "Let them go."

"I got to see, Lieutenant."

"Downtown," DeVasto said. "Later."

"Christ, DeVasto! She's my wife!"

The lieutenant watched Harry Schott, then nodded to the medical examiner's men. They set the body bag on the floor, opened it. Harry Schott looked down at the face of the dead woman, the face of his wife, the dead eyes filled with fear.

"We ain't got nothing worth stealing," Schott said.

I told him what had happened. More or less. The simple facts without the sounds I had listened to in the bathroom. Schott blinked at me, turned toward DeVasto.

"He was here? This guy? While—"

"In the bathroom, Harry. Locked in. He's got no weapon. Nothing he could have done."

"I'm sorry, Mr. Schott," I said.

"Them two?" Schott said. "Campbell and that Helen Kay? We got no addresses on them two. What do we know about them two?"

"She got scared, Mr. Schott," I said. "She panicked."

Schott said, "We don't know where them two are."

"She panicked, Harry," DeVasto said. "Started yelling for you, for the cops. Yelling for help."

"Why didn't she just let them look around?" Schott said. "I mean, why'd she try to stop him?"

"He scared her, Harry," DeVasto said.

"Who, Lieutenant?" Schott said. "Who was he, Lieutenant? Who is he?"

"We don't know," DeVasto said. "Not yet. But we will, Harry. We'll find out who he is, and we'll get him."

Harry Schott looked down at his wife. Then at me. Then at Lieutenant DeVasto. "How? No one saw him. He had no real reason to kill her. I mean, he killed her like some people kill flies. How're you gonna get him?"

"We'll get him," I said. "If not for your wife's murder, for another."

"You won't even ever know for sure he killed her," Schott said. "If you find him. You won't never know for sure *he* killed her. She just got killed. That's all you're ever gonna know for sure. Some guy just passed through and killed her."

The medical examiner's men had the body bag zipped up again, carried it out of the office. Harry Schott walked out behind them. Lieutenant DeVasto took the reports of his men, of his laboratory teams. They left to make their official reports or work on other details. DeVasto shrugged to me.

"All kinds of fingerprints, not much else. We'll run down the prints. If the guy's a pro he could be on file somewhere, but I wouldn't count on it. It won't help anyway. He'll have a cover story, and we've got no witnesses so far. The motel's about empty, no one saw anyone coming or going. They didn't even see you. Harry Schott's right, we'll never get him for this one."

"For something else, then," I said. "Okay if I go?"

DeVasto nodded. "Keep us on tap, okay? This looks like it got nothing to do with Derry City, a killer just passing through, but you never know. We been keeping gambling out, but it'll come in sooner or later, and a lot of people want it sooner. This could be tied to gambling, so when you get a good idea who it was, tell us, okay? At least we can try to place him in the city at the time, help you nail him.''

I took his card, thanked him, and went out into the afternoon, dark now with a steady rain. In my rented car I drove over the bridge and across the salt marshes behind the barrier beaches and turned north. I drove watching the endless flat sweep of the pine barrens, the vast emptiness of the bleak landscape in the driving rain. I could have tried to save her. It wouldn't have helped, and I'd probably have died with her, but I could have tried. All my judgment and experience told me I couldn't have saved her, and would have gotten myself killed, but I should have tried. That was what I should have done.

And I drove out of the pine barrens and into the rolling hills of central New Jersey and on toward the factories of the North. The rain fell hard and constant. With any luck I'd hit the Holland Tunnel by 4:00 P.M.

SIXTEEN

NUMBER 517 Perry Street was a low four-story Georgian-style brownstone around the corner from Hudson Street. Its original front steps had been removed, and Sarah Borden had the ground floor rear, the garden apartment. At just after 4:00 P.M. there was no answer to my ringing. Mail was still inside her lobby box. I could stake out or go on up to my office and return later. A single girl in New York might not come home all night. I left a note in her mailbox telling her to call me.

I returned the rented car, and walked through the rain to my side-street office/apartment. I thought about the dead woman in Derry City, the dead fast-food store owner in Livingston, and the dog thrown off the roof. What was I into? What were Alan and Helen Kay Campbell into? What was Ian Campbell not telling me? I had no answers, not yet, and picked up my mail on the way up to my third-floor office in the old loft building. The mail didn't have any answers either.

At my desk I called my answering service. They didn't have the answers, but they had a message. A Kay Michaels had called. She was in town from California, would I care to call her at 687-4422. I cared. Kay Michaels was a model and actress I'd met on my last trip to California. It had been nice in California. I called the number. There was no answer. It was becoming a bad day all around. Then, maybe it was for the best. With the pain still hammering at my kidneys, tomorrow could be better for Kay Michaels.

I got back into my duffel coat and beret and went out to walk uptown to the laboratory where they were analyzing the scrapings from Alan Campbell's bedroom floor. The rain had all but stopped, the blackest storm clouds passing to the south of the city and on out to sea, a colder wind blowing in from the west. At the laboratory they had the results, but still had to have them certified and sealed by the boss. I cooled my heels until the boss, Dr. Julian Cook, came out with the envelope.

"How much do I pay for the seal and signature?"

"Plenty," Cook grinned. "Authentic and untouched by outside hands, Danny boy."

"I'll break the seal at home. How about a hint now that I've paid the ransom?"

"Motor oil."

"Motor oil?"

"Motor oil. Type used a lot in motorcycles. A good-sized leak or a vehicle in one spot for some time."

I walked back downtown to my apartment thinking about a large stain of motor oil on a bedroom floor in a suburban house. Probably from a motorcycle. In the bedroom. I was still thinking about the oil and the bedroom, halfway up the last flight to my floor, when I heard the noise inside my office/apartment. I stopped, listened. Someone was inside. Again. Opening desk drawers. Quiet, but not quiet enough.

I could break the door down this time. A second chance. With less reason to break it down now than in Derry City, and just as much risk.

I went up past my door and continued on all the way to the roof.

SEVENTEEN

THE RAIN HAD stopped, the clouds blowing rapidly away on the cold wind, the temperature dropping. There was no one on the roof, and no hooks or climbing equipment on the parapet. Below, my windows were all closed, back and front.

Softly, I slipped back down to my floor, used my ring of keys on my neighbor's apartment door. He worked afternoons and evenings, would not be at home, and if he was I'd explain. He wasn't. I left the door open a crack, settled down to wait.

No one came up or went down the stairs, the sounds of the city seemed far off. Only the dim silence of the landing and the stairwell fading downward. I became aware of the small sounds behind my own door along the landing. Paper rustling. The dull *thock* of wood against wood. The clink of glass against metal. Like listening to a cat play silently in the dark at night, a hidden rodent moving inside the walls.

A half an hour passed before I heard the footsteps coming toward the door from inside. Footsteps that stopped just behind the door. Listening for any sounds in the corridor. Careful. And the man who stepped out was no stranger. Tall, broad, and a touch heavy, with curly dark hair silver at the temples. The man in Alan Campbell's bedroom in Chatham—Steve Norris, vice-president for personnel and security at Computer Methods Corporation. When he turned to close the door, I stepped out behind him, my hand in the pocket of my duffel coat.

"Back inside."

He didn't turn. He didn't move at all.

"Hello, Fortune."

"Walk," I said.

He walked back into my apartment. A quick glance inside told me that he was pretty good at nosing around. My desk, the entire office section, was almost as neat and untouched as it had been last night when the dog killer had come in through the window. Almost, but not quite.

"Something special you wanted, Norris?"

His voice was light, bantering, "Anything about Alan Campbell."

"For his father," I said. "To help out. Family friend."

"And business associate."

"He sent you to see how I was doing. You let yourself in to wait, then got tired of waiting so left, right?"

"Something like that."

He wore a long, pile-lined jacket now, a dark cap and old gray slacks, and he had still not tried to turn. He had no way of knowing if I had a gun or not, did nothing to find out. Most men would have tried to turn, protest, explain. Amateurs will bluff and brazen, even try to fight. Norris had walked quietly back into the office and stood with his back to me the whole time we were talking. Only a trained man does that. An old cop, an ex-CIA man, a onetime FBI agent, something. Once you've been trained, you never lose it. He had once been something more than a businessman.

"Nothing like that," I said. I sat behind my desk. Norris still didn't turn. "Campbell didn't send you. It's too soon and not his style. He'll wait a reasonable time for me to call him. He didn't send you here, and he didn't send you to Alan's house out in Chatham. He never asked you to help. Whatever you're doing is on your own, and what are you really, Norris?"

Now he turned. I had changed the confrontation into an interrogation, and now he could turn without danger. You don't forget.

"I told you what I am: vice-president for personnel and security at Computer Methods Corporation, and a friend of Ian Campbell and his family."

"What were you before you were a vice-president?"

"You want my whole résumé? How many companies back?"

"No companies," I said. "Before the companies, before the businessman."

He watched me. "We've all been a lot of things. Student, soldier, trainee, you name it."

"Name me what trained you to deal with a gun in your back? Taught you how to search. Somewhere, sometime, you've been trained. A little out of practice, but it shows. What? CIA? FBI? MI-5? KGB? The police?"

He tried to laugh. "KGB? MI-5? What do you think Alan is, an international spy?"

"I don't know what Alan is, or you. What was it, Norris? Or what is it, maybe?"

He sat down on the edge of my desk, looked away toward the front windows overlooking Eighth Avenue. "CIA. A long time ago. CIA right out of college. Later I hooked up with New Jersey State Police. A couple of years. All a long time ago."

He gave me that cool grin. The one that revealed nothing.

"Now you're interested in Alan Campbell and his wife."

He leaned toward me, sincere and confiding. "Look, Dan, everything I told you out in Chatham was true, except that Ian didn't ask me to help. That's what has me worried. He should have asked me, he always does if he has some kind of personal problem. Something's wrong this time. I think it's bigger trouble than it looks, so I decided to try to help on my own. Ian *is* my friend."

His face was serious, earnest. Concerned and confiding in me. Giving me the full treatment: the sincere, honest family friend. His eyes gave him away. They watched me for a reaction, for the effect of his words on me. This didn't mean the words weren't true, only that at the moment he was more interested in making me believe him than in the truth.

"What kind of bigger trouble?" I said.

He sat back on the edge of my desk, ran his thick fingers through his graying hair. "Something more than Alan running off with some of his cash. Whatever it is, I think Ian needs help."

He sounded honest enough, but that went with the CIA training too. The story could be true, he had the feel of a man who liked to be in the action, or it could be a fairy tale for gullible half-wits. Or maybe a little of both.

"Something more than Campbell's told me?" I said.

"More than he's told anyone in Chatham," Norris said. "I don't know what he's told you."

I said nothing. Let him guess if I knew more than he did.

"Did you get that stain on the bedroom floor analyzed?" he said. "Was it blood?"

"Motor oil," I said.

"Motor oil?"

"Motor oil. The kind used in motorcycles."

"In the bedroom?"

I nodded. "That's what it looks like. A can of oil got spilled, or someone parked a motorcycle in the bedroom for at least a couple of days."

"Alan doesn't even have a motorcycle."

"Does Helen Kay?"

"I never saw her with one. Who the hell would park a motorcycle in a bedroom?"

"Especially in suburban New Jersey," I said.

I let him think about it for a while, and then my telephone rang. It was Sarah Borden.

"Mr. Fortune? You asked me to call?"

She had a nice voice, low and confident. She knew she had a nice voice. I guessed that she worked on the voice. Part of the game in the theater. Sometimes a voice is all you have to impress someone with. If the voice doesn't catch their interest, you may not get a second chance.

"I'd like to talk to you, Miss Borden."

"Is it about a job?"

"No, about Helen Kay Campbell and her husband."

She didn't miss a beat despite what must have been a disappointment. You have to develop a thick hide in any art.

"Of course. Say, Downey's Restaurant in half an hour?"

It was dinnertime. A free dinner is an extra day's pay.

"I know where it is," I said. "Half an hour."

I hung up. Norris got off my desk.

"Who's Miss Borden?" he asked.

"The name doesn't mean anything to you?"

"No. Should it?"

"She's an old friend of Helen Kay Campbell's."

"How old?"

I told him. About Flagstaff and Derry City.

"Can I come with you?"

"Why not?"

With a little luck, I could pass the dinner check on to him. The lower you can keep an expense account, the more you can pad it. We all learn how to survive in a money world.

EIGHTEEN

NORRIS HAD PARKED his old dark blue Mercedes convertible two-seater out of sight around the corner on Eighth Avenue. Another reflex of the trained agent, cop. The leather of the bucket seats massaged me as I got in. Soft and supple and cared for.

"Nice car," I said.

"I like it," Norris said, "my wife doesn't. Too old and too small. Not up to our place in the community."

We drove up Eighth Avenue. Norris sounded bitter about his wife. He liked his old car, but it wasn't a status symbol by current standards. Not where money, and the spending of money, was the only standard. In midtown we parked in a garage on Tenth Avenue and walked back to Eighth. The bouncer on the door of Downey's passed us in, and the captain took us to Sarah Borden in a booth. The row of booths had a full view of the front door. It was where you sat to see and be seen. I introduced Norris.

"Mr. Norris," Sarah Borden said.

She was a compact young woman in a high-necked black wool dress that was split up her thigh and left her arms and shoulders bare. Three-and-a-half inch heels gave her height and slimmed her ankles, and she had a good if not spectacular body. A smooth oval face that was alert and mobile with no strong features to draw attention. A pliant face that seemed to change quickly and often. Both body and face would be assets to an actress. Nothing extreme or limiting.

"Have I seen you in the movies?" Norris said as we slid into the booth facing her. "Maybe the theater? I feel I have."

"Not unless you haunt off-off-Broadway or watch a lot of television commercials," Sarah Borden said. But she smiled anyway. Any recognition is nice, even imaginary.

I ordered the drinks: Scotch for Norris, a Beck's for me, and Sarah Borden had a martini, very dry, on the rocks.

"What do you want to know about Helen Kay and Alan?"

"Have you seen them recently? Or heard from them?"

"Yes."

I sat forward. "Which?"

"Both."

"Where? When?"

The waiter brought our drinks. Sarah Borden stirred her martini. "Why do you want to know, Mr. Fortune?"

"Alan's father hired me to find them." I showed her my credentials. "They sold their house in Chatham, cashed in some bonds, and disappeared. Mr. Campbell's worried."

"Alan's a grown man."

"The house they sold wasn't really theirs. Alan cashed the bonds for a business venture but never joined the venture. He left his job without any notice. In other words they ran off with Mr. Campbell's money."

"That happens all the time," Sarah Borden said. "I left with the bank account my parents had saved, and the cash from a drawer of savings bonds. How else do we get started?"

She gave me a big smile. Sarah Borden would go far; you could feel it flowing from her. In the way she inspected the whole room in a slow sweep like a tank gunner searching for the enemy. The way she parried Norris's flirting with her, and enticed him at the same time.

"It's not exactly the same thing," I said. "Did you leave in a hurry while your parents were in Europe? Have you dropped out of sight? Are you hiding?"

"They're not hiding either," she said. "Not from me."

She gave me the smile again, finished her martini. I waved to the waiter for another round. Were they running only from Chatham and Ian Campbell? A domineering father and a dependent life? Just to be free and independent? Then who and what was the killer of the landlady and the fast-food owner? The waiter returned. Sarah Borden tasted her second martini. It seemed good.

"How much money did they leave with?" she asked.

"A lot. Why?"

"I wondered." She seemed to enjoy the bite of the gin. "They're so...what? Happy? Jubilant? On a summer vacation, not a care in the world. Almost the way it was in Derry City last year."

"Having fun?"

"Determinedly. Almost manic. Especially Helen Kay."

"As if she'd been held down, was breaking loose?"

"I'd say so. Like that anyway." She sipped, smiled, and picked up a menu. "Is anyone else hungry?"

"I could eat," Steve Norris said. He hadn't stopped watching her the whole time.

"It's that time," I agreed.

Sarah Borden ordered sautéed scallops, with a lobster cocktail first. Norris chose the filet. I had trout. We each had a third drink. Sarah Borden seemed to unwind with the third martini. Norris was still staring at her. The beer relaxed me too.

"Did they tell you anything about what they plan to do?" I asked.

"No. Helen Kay never was one for making plans. Take a trip, perhaps a lot of trips. Everywhere. We'd all meet out in California where I'd get bit TV parts and they'd have a

ball.'' She sipped, savored. "Helen Kay's not really very
smart. She never was. She had to quit school in ninth or
tenth grade. But she's shrewd enough. She gets what she
wants, can take care of herself.''

I remembered the photographs I had, Alan and Helen
Kay in front of the Shamrock last year. The wiry, street-kid
look of Helen Kay despite the magazine-cover face and the
curves.

"They gave no long-range plans? Only—"

Her eyes had started another slow survey of the room. She
put down her glass, and waved. "Jerry!"

A thin, dark man in a windbreaker and jeans had come
into the restaurant. Hunched inside his light clothes, he
looked toward Sarah Borden. He didn't smile. She got up.

"I'll be right back.''

The thin man had turned into the bar. Sarah Borden followed him. Steve Norris stared at the spot where she had
vanished around the partition into the bar.

"That's some woman,'' Norris said.

For the first time I sensed the restlessness about him. It
could explain some things. Restless. Ripe for adventure,
action, change. Something pacing behind his eyes.

"Trouble,'' I said.

"What isn't that's worth chasing?''

Not much, I could have said, but he'd supply his own
clichés, his own encouragement. The waiter brought her
lobster cocktail, asked if we were ready for our dinners. I
told him to wait a few minutes. Sarah Borden didn't come
back.

"Hold the fort,'' I told Norris.

I walked to the back of the row of booths, looked around
the partition into the rear of the bar. Sarah Borden sat at the
bar, the dark young man beside her. Her hand rested on his
arm. The young man smiled, but there wasn't much happi-

ness in it. I moved closer, bent over the cigarette machine. They weren't concerned with me or with anyone.

"Could we, Jerry?" Her voice was as soft now as her smile. "Try again? Could we?"

"Why?"

"It just happened." Her hand squeezed his arm. "I didn't plan it that way, Jerry. I mean, Sally happened to you."

"Something did."

"Please," Sarah Borden said. "Come and see me? Sunday. Come on Sunday. The afternoon. We'll talk. We could always talk, couldn't we?"

"Could we?" There was more than a little bitterness in Jerry's voice, yet there was a thickness too, like blood swelling his throat. Her hand moved on his arm, stroking.

"We had good times. All the good times. Come on Sunday."

He was a former lover, an ex-lover, a lost lover. One of those or all three, and it was clear in her bright, sad eyes, and his long, tense face who had ended it. Yet she had been eager, even fervent when she had seen him come in. After how long? A year? A month? A week? A day? More than a year? There was no way to tell. Two years or two weeks, there isn't much difference when you're young and vulnerable. Not either way. Two weeks can be two years, two years two weeks. Instant change and memory forever.

"I don't know, Sarah," Jerry said.

"Please?"

Why was there such a sense of loss between them? Because they were young and dreamers? With the need to rush on, yet the need to lose no one? A transient world of dreams and ambition, and something has to endure.

"Sunday?" he said. "In the afternoon?"

He knew she meant nothing more. Sunday, in the afternoon. He knew too that he would go on Sunday. In the af-

ternoon. Sunday was Sunday. Monday was Monday. People
who live for tomorrow need to keep yesterday.

"All right," Jerry said.

Behind them a middle-aged bartender polished the same
glass for the fifth time. He wore a sensible sweater under his
green bartender's jacket, would be a man with a wife, children, and an old mother out in Queens. He would have been
born in Queens, married a girl from the same parish, spent
his life behind a bar watching the Sarah Bordens on their
way to success or failure. Each night he would take the subway home to Queens convinced of the truth and happiness
of his world, until the years passed and his sense of certainty somehow slipped away and he would never know
why. Would know only that the alive young people who
passed in front of his bar seemed to have something he did
not, and that he was less and less sure that he had ever lived
at all.

"Sunday." Sarah Borden smiled. "All afternoon."

The young man, Jerry, drank and left the bar. Sarah
Borden sat alone for a time. She saw the bartender watching, flashed her biggest smile and a small wink as she stood
up. I went back to the booth. She came around the front of
the partition. The waiter brought our delayed dinners. He
didn't seem surprised or annoyed, table-hopping was the
rule in a theatrical restaurant.

"Sorry," Sarah Borden said. "An old friend. First I had
in New York, but he'll never get anywhere. Poor Jerry."

"Does he know Helen Kay and Alan?"

"Jerry? God, no! Jerry's an intellectual, a writer, a
dreamer of perfect worlds. He doesn't know a thing about
people. Helen Kay'd scare him to death."

"Isn't Alan Campbell something like that?"

She ate her scallops, thought about it. "I suppose so. I'd
certainly have said so down there in Derry City last year. I
didn't give them six months, any more than I gave Darlene

and that Albano boy six months. It looks like I was wrong about Alan and Helen Kay. I suppose Alan really loves her.''

"Don't you think she loves him?"

"In her way, I suppose she does. She didn't grow up with much chance to learn about love, Mr. Fortune. Passed around from home to home all her life. A keep-quiet, eat-what-we-tell-you, wear-hand-me-downs life. It makes you tough when it works, but not much else.''

"It can make you grab hard for what you want," I said.

"It can do that," she agreed. "Is there—?"

She had finished her dinner, and the waiter appeared with a large piece of Sacher torte. She looked down at it, and then up at us. "It's my favorite dessert. Who knew?"

"I asked the waiter," Norris said.

She raised one of her thin, shaped eyebrows and smiled at him. She began to eat the rich chocolate cake slowly, as if she were tasting Norris's intentions. I waited for the coffee, sipped it when it came. It was good coffee.

"You were going to ask me a question," I said to Sarah Borden.

She nodded. "Is there something about Alan and Helen Kay you haven't told me yet? Some trouble?"

"Maybe trouble, maybe danger, maybe both," I said, and told her about the two murders. "The fast-food owner was supposed to go into business with Alan, and the killer of Mrs. Schott was looking for them." I described the small man and the big black who'd been at the bridge over the Passaic in front of Ian Campbell's house. "They ring any bells?"

She finished her Sacher torte, drank her coffee. "I don't think so." She drank again. "My God, Mrs. Schott? Why? I saw Alan and Helen Kay last only a few days ago. They didn't act as if they were in any danger. Having fun, on a big lark.''

"You saw them here in town?"

"Yes. In a Village tavern."

"You know where they're living?"

"The Hotel Emerson on West Forty-eighth Street."

I finished my coffee. She had taken long enough to tell me they weren't much more than around the corner from Downey's. Because she had wanted to get her free dinner first, or some other reason? I stood up, nodded to Norris.

"Pay the check."

I hurried out. Behind me I saw Norris reach for his wallet, a little surprised. I saw Sarah Borden put her hand on his arm, squeeze lightly, and smile at him.

NINETEEN

THE HOTEL EMERSON was halfway up the dim block between Sixth and Seventh avenues, a frigid wind now blowing along the block from river to river. Few people passed here; the crowds were back on Times Square. The few who did were bent into the wind or blowing with it.

The Hotel Emerson was a Victorian pile of blackened stone and gingerbread carvings with a fire escape in front. The street-floor windows were painted black, had faded gilt lettering that offered real estate and tax consultation on one side of the lobby entrance, adult books and magazines on the other.

The lobby itself was carpeted in an oriental pattern that had acquired a smooth surface of blackish gray over the years. A half century or more of city air had caramelized the white walls. There were faded overstuffed chairs and couches framed by nameless potted plants, and faded people who sat on them silently watching anyone who came in or went out. The registration desk was an ornate relic with the soft shine of a million sleeves.

"Mr. and Mrs. Alan Campbell?" I asked the clerk.

"That'll be four-oh-eight, but they ain't in. You want to leave a message?"

"No."

I looked at my watch. It wasn't quite 9:00 P.M. yet. There was a cocktail lounge through the door at the left of the lobby. As I headed toward it, Steve Norris came into the lobby. He saw me, came to join me.

"Make out okay?" I said.

He smiled. "I have to call her in an hour."

The cocktail lounge was long and narrow, with another entrance from the street. We took a back booth from where we could see the lobby and the street entrance. I went for the drinks. The bartender was a lumpy man with dull eyes. I ordered a Scotch and a bottle of Schlitz and showed him my photos of Alan and Helen Kay.

"Sure, they comes in regular."

"Today?"

"Not so far. Sometimes they goes away. When they're here, they comes in."

Norris looked at his watch as I set down his Scotch, slid into the booth with my Schlitz. He still had fifty minutes to go. An anxious man ready for some action. If he looked at his watch every two minutes it was going to be a long fifty minutes. I gave him some help.

"How long have you known Campbell and his family?"

"Since I joined the company."

"How long is that?"

"Seven years, give or take."

"Vice-president from the start?"

"No, we never had corporate officers except Ian and Turk Aherne. Just department heads until about a year ago. Now we've got a fistful of vice-presidents. Ian's a man who likes power over the lives of people who work for him. He made vice-presidents out of some of the department heads and assistants, left others with the same titles right where they were. Some of them quit, and he's been letting others go all year. Mostly the older people. I think because the younger guys are more dependent on Ian for their jobs."

"What does the partner, Aherne, think about all that?"

"Turk's not too happy."

"Why didn't he stop the reshuffle then?"

"I think he tried. Ian did it one man at a time, and I heard that Turk opposed every one. It didn't do any good. When it comes down to the mat, Ian's got the power."

"What about before this year? How did Campbell and Aherne get along?"

We both watched the open door into the lobby and the street door. Norris continued to look at his watch.

"Okay as far as I know. Not exactly the best of friends. Turk's more down-to-earth, gets along with all kinds of people. Ian's something of a snob, Main Line manners and Ivy League class. The staff like Turk better. Turk's a better salesman, and knows more about computers too, but Ian's good with corporate deals and money. Outside they never seemed to mix much."

"Campbell only socializes with the daughter," I said.

"That's pretty recent," Norris said, looked at his watch again. He was down to fifteen minutes. "And Leah's a lot more sophisticated than her parents. Went to Smith, picked up the good manners and the class."

"How about you?"

"Me?"

"How do you get along with Campbell and Aherne?"

"At work, fine. Mine's the kind of job that doesn't get in anyone's way. I step on no toes. Outside I don't see Turk. I see Ian as much as anyone, I suppose. Dartmouth, football, the CIA. I guess I belong with Ian."

He didn't sound too happy about it, drank his Scotch absently, his mind somewhere else. He looked at his watch, shrugged.

"At least my wife is sure we belong with Ian. Turk's too low class. She's as much of a snob as Ian." He drank, and shook his head. "No, that's not fair or even true. She's just more comfortable with Ian and his circle, and so am I. We do belong with Ian, God help us."

He looked at his watch once more, and it was time. He headed into the lobby toward the pay phones. I went on watching the lobby and the street door of the crowded lounge, ordered another beer. I was feeling thirstier than I had in a long time. I knew why. Maybe I should call Kay Michaels again. The older you get, the more you find your comforts, your involvements where you can. Like locating a saloon with fifty different kinds of beer, and going each Friday night to try a different beer. It gives you something to look forward to. But a woman is better.

"I'm going to meet her." Norris stood over the booth. "I probably won't be too long, she's got something to do later. If you find Alan and Helen Kay, leave a note with the bartender, okay? I'll find you."

I nodded, watched him walk away toward the street door. He walked fast. He wanted to be with me when I found Alan and Helen Kay, maybe to talk to Alan before Ian Campbell did. Maybe that was what Ian Campbell didn't want. I wondered if Norris was all the loyal friend and employee he made out to be? Whatever, he wanted to find Alan, but he seemed to want a woman more. A new woman. An adventure.

I finished my beer, ordered another, went on watching the lobby. The old hotel was home to the overage loners who lived in it year in and year out, to the transients who arrived in the city on buses with everything they owned in a single suitcase. The people the census taker misses. The re-

verse coin of free enterprise. The losers. I ordered another
beer.

I still had half this last beer when I saw them.

TWENTY

THEY CAME ACROSS the seedy lobby hand in hand like two
kids playing in the sun. Laughing as if they had nothing on
their minds but their own high spirits. Maybe they hadn't.
Maybe I was the guilty one, spying on them.

They seemed out of place among the old and forgotten,
striding across the lobby and into the lounge where Alan got
two beers at the bar and they sat at a corner table in the
shadows, bent close and still laughing. Only their clothes
fitted with the seedy hotel—torn, stained jeans; grimy work
shirts; worn baseball jackets; run-down and scuffed boots.
Outcasts like the others in the hotel. Only for them it was a
choice. The country had no place for the others; they had no
place for the country.

"Hello, Alan." I stood over their table. "Helen Kay."

She put her hand on his arm. He raised his head slowly to
look at me.

"Do we know you?"

"No, but I know you." I sat down at the table. "Dan
Fortune. Your father hired me to find you, tell him where
you are, bring you home if I could."

"Father?" Helen Kay said. "You mean Ian sent you?"

Alan took a long drink of his beer. "Okay, so you found
us. Hey, what are you, a private eye?" He laughed.

Helen Kay took her hand away from his arm. Up close the
shabby clothes did nothing to hurt her looks or her figure.
The large breasts stretched the denim work shirt, and the
round hips filled the jeans. The shirt and tight jeans en-

hanced her small waist and flat belly. She'd let her dark hair
grow longer, but had chopped it off halfway down her slim
neck. With her flawless face, pouting lips, and belligerent
eyes, the ragged hair gave her that strange mixture of fashion model and street punk. The clothes were all punk, yet I
had the feeling she knew the power of her looks.

"Right out of the movies," I said. "You want to come
back to Chatham and tell your father why you left?"

Alan had the same lank blond hair and thick mustache
from the photos a year ago and two months ago. Almost the
same clothes and the same bland face, but his eyes were less
anxious. His eyes almost as belligerent as Helen Kay's, and
his smile now intended to please no one. The year hadn't
changed his appearance much, but it had his manner. A lot
more confident, even arrogant. I didn't have to look far for
the source of the change.

"Why should we?" Helen Kay said.

"What do you say, Alan?" I said.

"Why should we?" Alan said.

"You cashed in bonds by lying about an investment, you
sold a house at a loss that wasn't really yours to sell."

"He gave us the house," Helen Kay said. "We found a
better deal to put the cash in."

"What deal?"

"That's our business," she said. "Hey, c'mon, relax, you
know? I mean, are you really a private eye? You carry a gun
'n' all? I bet you got some great stories, right?"

Her eyes were big and eager and I didn't think it was an
act. She gave me a nice smile, a pout, and a lot of eye contact. That was an act, and a good one. I felt it down to my
shoes. She was a combination of spontaneity and calcula-
tion that wasn't going to be easy to work with.

"Why don't you want to live in Chatham?"

"Because it's a drag. God, is it ever a royal drag!" She
finished her beer. "Hey, I'm tired of this place and my feet

hurt. You want to talk, come on up to the room. I got to get
these boots off. Buy us all a couple of beers, private eye, and
we'll go on up."

Everyone's a hustler these days.

I bought six bottles at the bar, left a note for Steve Norris. The bartender didn't like us bypassing room service, but
Helen Kay flashed him one of her pouts and smiles and his
eyes watched us all the way across the lobby to the elevator.
Even a bartender can dream.

The rickety elevator let us off in a dim corridor. Alan led
the way along the dusty carpeting to room 408.

It was a small room with two curtainless windows. The
bed was unmade, looked as if there had been a war in it.
There probably had been, but a war of needs and pleasures
nobody lost as long as the needs were real. Empty fast-food
containers littered the single bureau, two backpacks stood
open but still packed on the floor. There was a tall wardrobe against the wall opposite the bed. The hotel was too old
to have closets in every room. There were three hard, up-
holstered chairs, and that was all. Alan opened three of the
beers. Helen Kay kicked off her boots, sat on the bed rubbing her feet, and leaned toward me over her beer bottle.

"You ever worked for your old man, private eye? You
ever marry a man who lived in the same town as his old
man, worked for his old man, even lived in a house the old
man bought him?"

"No," I said. I sat in one of the hard chairs, drank my
beer.

"No," she said. "Well, I took it as long as I damn could,
believe me. Alan took it until he'd got it to his ass, up and
down. No more, you know? No way, Jose!"

She was fierce and challenging me. The way it had to be,
what she had to do. The judgment of youth, total and
maybe excessive, but not criminal. Black and white, and I
knew who was the power of the pair. Alan sat on one of the

other hard chairs and slowly picked the label off his beer bottle. He piled the pieces neatly into a small mound of debris on the chair arm. I wondered if he'd only changed one tyrant for another.

"Ian paid him okay," I said. "He gave you a house."

"Give and take back," Helen Kay said. "A handout and a fist. Jump, boy!"

Alan said, "I had to want what he wanted me to want."

They were working as a team. At least for the moment. Solid in their closeness and their views. Alan had even begun to imitate her western style of speech.

"So you just want out of Chatham, away from Ian," I said.

"As far as we can get," Helen Kay said.

"And as fast," Alan said.

I said, "And do what?"

"Anything we want to do," Helen Kay said.

"As long as it ain't in some office," Alan said.

"Something you can feel, you know?" Helen Kay said. She jumped off the bed, whirled in a circle with her bottle of beer, dancing with the bottle.

"Outdoors," Alan said. "Get your back and muscles in it."

"Only first we're gonna take a trip," Helen Kay said. She sat back down on the bed, her feet tucked up under her Indian fashion, body erect with the breasts thrust out and high, the belly flat, sitting on the curve of her thighs and buttocks. Erotic and young at the same time. That mixture again. As old as time and a child of impulse. "A real long trip on our bikes. Everywhere the damn bikes can take us, you know?" Excitement in her voice, her eyes seeing great distances, feeling the wind on her face.

"Motorcycles?" I said.

She nodded, happy. "We got two brand new Harleys! No damn little Jap bikes. Harleys with *everything* on them, you know? You can *live* on them if you got to."

"Even park them in the bedroom?"

She bounced on the bed. "Hey, I mean, sometimes I just got to look at my bike. I got to know it's *there*, right? I gotta know I can just get on it and *go*!"

"I didn't know you were into motorcycles," I said to Alan.

She looked toward him where he was at work on his second bottle of beer, drinking it and pulling off the label again. He continued to pile the torn debris of the label into the small mound on his chair arm, and looked toward her.

"I guess I turned him on about bikes," she said. "Ain't that right, honey?"

"That's right," he agreed. "We're going to get old like you and my father soon enough. Then the fun's over, so now's the time to live it all."

"On your father's money," I said.

Helen Kay was off the bed again. A girl who couldn't stay still for long at any given time. "He *gave* us the house, and those bonds was Alan's! If he had strings in his mind that's his prob, you know? He put strings on, all bets're off."

"No obligations at all," I said.

"Alan don't owe him nothing."

I said, "Not even a little talk before you walked out? At least come out in the open and tell him what you wanted to do and why? Give him a chance to understand?"

They each sucked on their second beers and looked surly. Alan looked a little uneasy too. Maybe he didn't really want to lose all ties with his father. Or all ties to his father's money. But his ties to Helen Kay were tighter. At least now.

"He'd never understand," Alan said.

"We don't owe him nothing," Helen Kay repeated.

I said, "I suppose that means you don't want to go back to Chatham and explain it all to him?"

"We ain't never going back to that place," Helen Kay said.

"And we're not going to explain anything to my father," Alan said.

They were sure about that. Definite. Nothing was going to get them back to Chatham, or make them talk to Ian Campbell, and maybe they were too definite. Were they so afraid Ian Campbell would get the money back and block them from freedom and their motorcycles, or was there something else? Something more dangerous?

"Are you going to explain what happened to the bond money that was a better deal than Livingston Mall?"

Alan said, "Helen Kay told you that was our business."

"Why should we?" Helen Kay said.

"Because," I said, "if you don't you could end up part of murder."

"Murder?" Helen Kay leaned back against the bed, drank from her bottle.

"Murder?" Alan stopped tearing the label from his bottle.

I had their attention, and the shock was real. Yet I had a feeling they were not all that surprised. As if they had not exactly expected murder, but had been aware of the possibility. Aware of some kind of risk, of some danger. Of something that made murder less than a bolt from the blue.

"Andrew Katz, the man you were going into business with, Alan, was killed in his shop in Livingston Mall. Mrs. Schott, your landlady at the Shamrock Motel, was killed down in Derry City. You know anything about either or both?"

They both watched me as if they expected me to go on, to tell them something more. They waited, then looked at each other, and, after a time, shook their heads.

"Why would anyone want to murder Katz?" Alan said.

"Or old lady Schott?" Helen Kay said.

"You don't have any idea at all?"

They both shook their heads again.

"It couldn't have some connection to what you did with that bond money? Maybe the house money too? The better deal?"

"No," Alan said.

"Look," Helen Kay said, "we bought the Harleys with that bond money, okay? The Harleys and a lot of travel stuff. We never was gonna invest it in that fast-food deal, that was just so the old man would give us the okay. We bought the Harleys, the rest of the cash we still got. I mean, it's our stake when we head west, right?"

"Two motorcycles and travel money," I said.

"You can check it out," Alan said.

"I can, and the police can," I said. "Okay, I'll buy that. Both Mrs. Schott and Katz were knifed. By someone who knows how to cut quick and quiet. The killer who got Mrs. Schott was looking for Helen Kay. I think the guy who murdered Katz may have been too. Does any of that ring a bell?"

"Me?" Helen Kay said. "Looking for me?"

"Why?" Alan said.

"How do you know he was looking for me?" Helen Kay said.

I told her about the small man and the big black in the leisure suit at Ian Campbell's house in Chatham. I told her what I had heard when the landlady was murdered. "Does any of that mean anything to you two? Those two men, do they ring a bell?"

Helen Kay frowned, seemed to think. "No, not a thing."

"No way," Alan said.

For the first time I had the feeling they were lying. Or at least Helen Kay was. The quick, restless girl wasn't the thinking type. Until now she'd answered everything fast and without thinking a whole lot, without frowns to show how hard she was thinking about my questions. I had the definite feeling that she knew the two men I'd seen at the stone bridge in Chatham—and maybe later—or knew about them.

"Hey," she said, finished her beer, "all this talk's makin' me thirsty as hell. Let's all go on back down and get another couple o' beers."

"I could handle another or three," Alan said.

"Split my second one," I said. "You know, the two of you might be better off back in Chatham. A lot safer anyway. At least for a while."

Alan opened my last beer, drank, passed it on to Helen Kay. She drank a long gulp, passed the bottle back.

"Why would we want to be safer?" she said.

"We got nothing to be scared of," Alan said, drank and passed again.

"And we ain't going back to Chatham," Helen Kay said.

They were making short work of the last bottle of beer.

"I can't force you," I said. "Look, Steve Norris should be up here soon. Maybe he can convince you to go back and at least talk to Ian. Who knows, maybe Ian would understand what you want, even come up with some more money."

"Norris?" Helen Kay said. "What the hell's he doing around here?"

"He's in the hotel?" Alan said.

"He will be, I left a note at the bar," I said. "He's been helping try to find you two. Maybe Chatham isn't that bad a place to live. People care about you."

"Shit! Norris works for Ian." Helen Kay swore. "No one cares about anyone except themselves. Hey, now we're all out of beer, and all this talking dries me out. You don't want us to go down to the bar, private eye, you better spring for some more bottles."

"I'll buy," I said, "if Alan goes down."

"You think we'd run out on you, private eye?" Helen Kay nodded to Alan. "Honey, go down, okay? The man's scared we'll take off on him, so don't go running away without me."

She laughed, and I gave Alan a twenty. The necessities get more expensive every year. Alan trotted after the beer and Helen Kay lit a cigarette. The necessities don't change, no matter what horrors we attribute to them. Need is greater than fear. It always has been, one way or another. And it was the first cigarette I'd seen her smoke.

"You like it?" she said. She was back on the bed, on the edge, swinging her legs and smoking. "Private snooping, I mean?"

"I like it," I said. "What about you? What do you want to do?"

"Hey, I don't know yet. I got plenty of time." She flashed me the smile and the pout. It was right out of a prime-time commercial, phony and dazzling. "It's dangerous, right? I mean, the detective stuff? That's the kicks, right? The risk and all?"

"It's better than a desk job," I said, "but the hours are long. You make a choice."

She frowned. "I don't like working long. I mean, I got a lot better things to do."

"Like riding a motorcycle?"

She nodded, blew a long stream of smoke. "Just go, you know? Fast and far." She frowned again, swung her leg. The frown seemed to be her one expression for any kind of thinking. "Bet you make real good money though. I mean, people got trouble, they're gonna pay plenty."

"Not as good as stealing," I said, "but steadier."

"Yeh," she said, but it was her own voice inside she was listening to not mine. "I mean, you get to know all about the trouble people got, you know? They tell you things, and you figures out other stuff, and pretty soon you know everything and then they really got to pay. I mean, if they don't—"

"Here! Helen Kay! Down by the elevator! Hurry!"

She was up and so was I. It was Alan's voice from somewhere outside along the corridor toward the elevator. Helen Kay was at the door.

"No," I said. "You stay out of sight."

She stepped back and I inched my head around the door frame and peered along the dim carpeted corridor. I saw nothing and no one.

"Helen Kay! Fortune! Hurry!"

At the far end of the corridor the elevator stood open. I saw nothing of Alan. Only his voice urgent from somewhere at that end of the silent hotel corridor. It was one of those few times when I wished I carried my old gun. But not really. A gun creates more danger than it protects against. I told myself that as I tried to move as quietly as a shadow along the corridor toward where the elevator stood open like the mouth of a mysterious tunnel full of unseen dangers beyond.

A tunnel that began to close as I reached it! And not empty. Alan Campbell stood inside the elevator grinning at me. As the doors closed he gave a small wave. The elevator started down. I looked for the stairs. He had been carrying no bottles, had obviously never gone down. If I hurried I might still . . .

I turned and ran back along the corridor to their room. It was empty. Swearing at myself, I ran down the corridor again in the opposite direction. Suckered by one of the oldest tricks in the book! The fire stairs door at this end of the corridor was open. I started down, listening. I heard nothing. When I reached the ground floor I hurried out into the lobby and across it to the street. I didn't see them anywhere

in the lobby. In the cold night street I looked both ways.
They were gone.

"Damn!"

The question was, why? I didn't have the answers, but I
had one answer—because there was more to their run-out
from Chatham and Campbell than two Harley-Davidsons
and a motorcycle trip. More than a footloose life and independence.

TWENTY-ONE

THE ONLY THING I could do beside wait in the bar for Steve
Norris was go back up to 408 and see if they'd left anything
behind that would give me a lead to where they might go
next.

I took the elevator this time—we're all getting older—and
heard movement far down the fourth-floor corridor and
inside the open door to 408.

At the open door I looked in—carefully.

A woman was walking around rapidly looking into the
wardrobe, behind the chairs, under the bed. She wore jeans,
a blue shirt, and boots just as Helen Kay had, but she wasn't
Helen Kay Campbell. The jeans were designer sleek, the
shirt would never know the meaning of work, and the boots
were high-heeled with the rich shine of glove-soft leather.
The woman was taller, her hair wasn't as dark and was long
on her shoulders, and she was a lot more chic and dazzling
if not as beautiful or spectacularly constructed. Helen Kay
didn't seem to want what she had been given except to use
it as a weapon. This woman enjoyed what she had and built
on it. Leah Aherne.

I stepped in. "What the hell are you doing here?"

"Mr. Fortune!" She turned quickly, but didn't back away. Startled but not fazed. She was a young woman who didn't faze easily, if at all, and who concentrated on her own concerns. "I think I saw Alan a few minutes ago in the lobby! He ran out before I could get close, and on the street I lost him."

"Did he see you?"

"I don't think so. Mr. Fortune, did I really see him? Was it Alan?"

"Maybe," I said. "I thought you didn't have any idea where Alan and Helen Kay were, or what they were doing, or why?"

She stood in the center of the small room now. She looked around her. She had already searched everywhere, and found nothing. Even the two backpacks were gone. Tall and slim, she still looked to me no more than twenty, but had the controlled poise of someone ten years older than her actual twenty-five years. The boyish face with its small nose and full lips was all business, as if she were on a mission.

"All right, Mr. Fortune, I'm looking for Alan and Helen Kay. When we talked I didn't know anything about where they were or what they were doing, but I did plan to try to find them."

"Why?"

"Because Ian has more on his mind than Alan. I know it. More than *just* Alan. Something that's worrying him too much."

"And that worries you."

"Yes, that worries me, Mr. Fortune."

"What happened to Dan?"

She smiled. "All right, Dan."

"This different worry. Could it involve your father?"

"I don't know. I have the feeling that it involves the company, and that would concern my father."

"And that's why you want to know about it? For your dad?"

"For Ian," she said. "I like Ian, and when you really like someone you owe them something. Ian's been strange lately sometimes. I have the feeling he has some big plans on his mind, and that something isn't working out right. I want to help, but he won't let me, won't tell me anything."

"Does your father know about the plans?"

"I don't know. I don't know if there really *are* any plans, but I know there's something wrong."

"How will finding Alan and Helen Kay help you?"

"I won't know until I find them. But, somehow, whatever's wrong is connected to Alan."

She half leaned, half sat against the top of the old bureau, and swung her leg. It seemed we were all getting the impression that Ian Campbell had more on his mind than an errant son.

"If you didn't know where Alan was yesterday, how did you track them here?"

"I went up to see Edna, Alan's mother, this morning. I had a hunch that if Alan was collecting money he wouldn't miss a try at his mother. Or Helen Kay wouldn't."

"She'd seen them?"

"Twice. The last time only a week ago. They gave her the address of this hotel."

"Weren't they afraid she'd tell Ian Campbell?"

"Not Edna, not if they told her they'd run out on him. She'd have enjoyed that. Anyway, they had to because she was supposed to send them a check."

She laughed and I heard the man walking along the corridor. I pulled her into the shadow of the wardrobe. The man walked into the room slowly, peering around.

"Fortune?"

It was Norris. I stepped out.

"How'd you make out?"

Norris looked past me into the shadows behind the tall wardrobe. "Who's that? Helen Kay? You found them?"

"I found them, but that's not Helen Kay." I told him what had happened in the room. "Suckered me good and flew away."

Leah Aherne came out of the shadows. "Mr. Norris."

"Miss Aherne?" Norris was confused.

"She's looking for Alan too," I said.

"Ian sent you to find Alan?" Norris asked.

"Not exactly," the girl said.

"Another volunteer," I said. "How'd you do with Sarah Borden?"

"All right," Norris said. "What did Alan and Helen Kay say to you before they ran off?"

I told him what they'd said to me.

"That's all? Be on their own away from Ian? So why not just tell Ian? And why run away from you tonight?"

"Motorcycles?" Leah Aherne said. "I never heard of Alan riding a motorcycle. He hates speed. I could never get him to ride in my Porsche."

Norris nodded. "I never heard of Alan liking any kind of machine. Not even a car."

"I guess Helen Kay changed him," I said. "And I can understand why they wouldn't want to tell Campbell they wanted to get out of Chatham and away from him. Especially with the money. I'm not sure why they ran away from me tonight."

Leah Aherne and Norris were silent in the empty hotel room. A neon sign from somewhere down on the street flashed from time to time. The traffic from both Broadway and the avenues below beat the night like the pulse of the city. There was a stiffness between Leah Aherne and Norris, like two strangers from the same country meeting abroad. Maybe it was the difference in status around Computer Methods Corporation, or the difference in position.

Daughter of one boss and doxy of the other. Their different interests. It certainly wasn't the difference in age for either of them.

Norris said, "Did Ian say anything about Alan or trouble in the company while you were in Europe?"

"No," Leah Aherne said. "We don't talk about company business, Mr. Norris."

"What do you talk about?" Norris said.

"What do you talk about to your wife?" Leah said.

"My wife and I don't talk about much of anything these days."

"I'm sorry."

"I'm not," Norris said. "We've got nothing to talk about."

"How sad," Leah said.

Norris was as restless as a wolf in a cage on a hot day. Looking for something, and not just a sexual adventure. Only it looked as if a quick romance would at least help, especially with a younger woman. Much younger. A challenge.

"I am sure of one thing," I said. "Alan and Helen Kay really don't want to go back to Chatham or talk to Campbell. We'll have to find them again and hold them. Any ideas from either of you about where they might go now?"

They both shook their heads.

"Okay," I said. "I'll have to think about what I'm going to do next, and if either of you think of anything call me."

"I will," Leah Aherne said.

Norris nodded.

I watched them. "Remember something, we're not the only ones looking for them. Somewhere we've got a killer who wants to find them. I don't know who it is or why he wants them, but he's out there looking too. If you learn anything, call me. Understand?"

Leah nodded.

"I'll follow Miss Aherne home before I drive back to Chatham," Norris said.

Leah Aherne did not object, and I watched them leave smiling. They were both restless looking. I wondered if one or both of them had found something that involved Alan Campbell? If there was more to their search for Alan and Helen Kay than some friendly help?

While I thought about that I searched the small room. The neon flashed on and off down in the street, the traffic and crowd noise throbbed in the distance. I found nothing. Helen Kay had even had time to grab the backpacks while I was down the hall on the snipe hunt they'd set up for me. Ian Campbell was not going to be pleased.

Down in the street I realized that Norris's going off after Leah Aherne had left me without a ride. Swell. I finally got a cab and rode down to my place. I decided not to tell Ian Campbell. But Norris would. I needed a drink. Or something.

In my apartment I called my answering service. Yes, they had another message from Kay Michaels. She missed me, call. I called. Again no answer. I watched an hour of bad television and called again. No answer. Independence has its disadvantages. I went to bed. Tomorrow I would get up early and fly to Syracuse. Alan's mother was the only real lead I had left.

TWENTY-TWO

THE ALLEGHENY AIRLINES 727 touched down in Syracuse just before noon. I rented a car, had lunch at a Mexican restaurant I'd discovered years ago just below where the university stands on its hill above the city. It's one of the few places I know away from the border where you can get real

Mexican food outside Mexico. I had the chicken *mole*, two beef enchiladas, and three bottles of Tres Equis beer.

The former Edna Campbell, now Killian, lived north of the city in what had been an isolated village in Colonial times but was now a suburb with tract developments bursting out of the woods like Joseph Brant and his Mohawks in those bloodier days. Today's developers had done what the Mohawks never could, destroyed the village. Mile after mile of identical driveways and packaged shopping centers surrounding the old frame and brick mansions of the nineteenth-century local tycoons, those rapacious Jacksonians who believed with a more recent California senator that real freedom was a man's right to have anything he could steal fair and square, to grab for himself in a dog-eat-dog fight with no namby-pamby responsibility for the losers or the lame.

The Killians' stately relic was on the village square, boxed in by tracts behind and the once open village common in front, the patch of grass fenced now to discourage undesirables from having picnics. An ungainly pile of red brick and white wood, three stories high with a slate roof and a porte cochere over a semicircular driveway. It stood on a small plot, well tended but unimpressive by today's standards. In New York of the late nineteenth century, town land had been too valuable to waste on privacy and lawn parties. There was a sense of nervous belt-tightening about the big old house. A broken pane in a living room bay window. Corroded patches of rust on the rain gutters and downspouts. Flaking white paint. And in the open six-car garage beside the house only two cars: a small MG two-seater, and a 1980 BMW sedan. I checked the license in my notebook. It was Alan Campbell's car.

A black maid answered the door. She took my name and business to Mrs. Killian, returned and led me through a large, formal entry hall of Wedgwood blue and white with a Federalist staircase curving upward on the right. A velvet-and-brocade living room opened through double doors to the left, and a mahogany-and-crystal dining room to the right. The maid took me to a glassed-in sun porch that overlooked the rear yard. Behind a high brick wall, there was no basketball hoop or barbecue in this backyard.

"Mr. Fortune," the maid announced in a flat voice. She sounded as if she didn't much like her employer.

Edna Killian didn't appear to care whether the maid liked her or not. A small, middle-aged woman, her round face was framed by short, matronly graying hair. She sat at a wicker table cutting and eating a pear with a silver knife. She wore a slim blue robe that matched her eyes. The eyes were quick and firm, even hard, and so was her voice.

"You're a private detective?"

I nodded. "I'm working for Ian Campbell. If—"

"Ah?" She shook her head. "I should never have left Ian. But how could I know he'd make that big a success?" She ate a slice of pear. "Now Killian's off trying to plug the leaks in our dike. You put people into government and they turn on you, forget what they're in government for. We got them in and now no more contracts. It wouldn't be proper. Proper!" She sliced the pear, ate. "I was sure Ian and that Aherne person would just limp along out there in Chatham, and Killian was a man who knew how to play all the angles. You simply never know, do you? You really can't count on anyone or anything these days."

She ate another slice of pear, seemed to think about all the people and things one couldn't count on. She appeared to have forgotten me. I waited, looked around the porch, which was warm in the November sun. A door was open into what looked like a large guest suite with bedroom and sitting room, a sunken tub in a large bathroom, and another glassed-in porch at the side of the house. The king-sized bed was violently unmade, and on the side porch a muscular young man in his early twenties was doing calisthenics in only a pair of jockey shorts.

"You enjoy young women, Mr. Fortune?"

Edna Killian had remembered me, watched me with a thin smile.

"When they let me. Mostly in passing these days."

"You get nothing in this world by watching it pass," Edna Killian said. "Where do you think I'd be if I'd waited for that boy in there to seduce me. He has no technique, an absolute primitive, but that's what I want, isn't it? The whole thing. The ignorance or stupidity or courage to have only your own truth no matter what anyone else tells you. The incipient robber baron with the whole world still ahead of him. Young." She finished her pear in two quick slices, carefully dried the silver knife. "If you're working for Ian, you must have come to ask me about Alan."

"Have you seen him recently? Or them?"

"Only a week ago," she said. She watched through the open bedroom door to where the young man was doing fluid sit-ups. "I hadn't seen Alan in years. My fault. Terry and Ron, my other boys, were almost grown before Ian and I split, and I had the girls up here once or twice, but I don't think Alan ever came up. He was just so young. Still, I rather like him now. He's grown into a lively boy with a lot of confidence and drive. That wife of his too. A strong girl."

"You knew they'd run out on Ian?"

"I knew they'd left Chatham. Ian called me a month or two ago. I hadn't seen them then, of course, and told Ian so. I also told him that Alan was, after all, married, and that he, Ian, always did like to run the entire show and that perhaps Alan had simply grown up. Ian wasn't too pleased with that." She laughed. "He told me about the house and the bonds, and I thought his reaction was excessive and told him so. After all, Alan's not just any boy, he's accustomed to certain needs."

"You didn't tell Ian when Alan came up here?"

"Alan asked me not to."

"Yet you told Leah Aherne."

"Alan didn't ask me not to. Besides, I like Leah, if not her family. Too much bowling and pastel pants suits."

"Isn't telling Leah the same as telling Ian?"

She found a cigarette in the pocket of her blue robe. In the bedroom suite the young man was examining his muscles. She lit the cigarette. "All right, you know about that. I told Leah because she thinks something more than Alan leaving home is going on, and if it is I'd like to know too. Alan didn't tell me anything about that possibility."

"Or maybe you want Ian to know where Alan is," I said.

She smoked. "Why would I want that? No, don't tell me any more. I can see you have a mind almost as devious as mine, so you must know that if I were hiding anything, and you came close to it, I'd only lie anyway."

"The way someone lies is pretty revealing," I said, and smiled. "You have no idea of what 'more' could be going on?"

"No, but I assume it's connected to the company."

"And you think Ian's becoming a big success?"

"It seems that way, Mr. Fortune."

"What did Alan want when he came here?"

She laughed again. "Money, of course. I hope to see me and show me his new wife too, but primarily it was money. They told me they'd invested all their capital and needed travel money to tide them over. They probably conned me, but that's all right, shows enterprise."

"How much did you give them?"

"Not much, a thousand or so. Just what I had on hand. Oh, I bought their car too. The price they wanted was just too good to refuse, and he *is* my son." She smiled.

"Since Ian paid for it, nobody lost," I said.

She stubbed out her cigarette, watched the muscular kid on the distant side porch. He was doing push-ups now, one arm at a time, still wearing only his jockey shorts. She watched him for some time. "I blew it with Ian, you know? Killian seemed like so much better a bet. That Aherne always thought small like most ordinary people, and I was sure Ian would always let him run the company. It seems I was wrong." She sighed. "From what Alan said Ian's a tougher businessman than I thought."

"How tougher?"

"Alan didn't go into any details." She lit another cigarette. "Killian hasn't been bad, but we do make mistakes, don't we?"

I wondered if maybe she had the idea of getting Ian Campbell back. After all, he had never remarried, and Alan was the last kid at home. Mistakes could be corrected.

"So a week ago was the last time you saw Alan?"

"Yes, but he called only this morning."

"From where?"

"Still New York."

"Why?"

"I still owe him half the money for the BMW, and he wanted to give me a new address. And he also wanted to know if anyone had been up here looking for them. Of course, you hadn't been here then, and no one else had, so I said no."

"What is his new address?"

She smoked. In the bedroom the young man was standing in the sunlight now, glistening with sweat like an oiled Roman gladiator. A living statue showing off his beautiful body. For Edna Killian or himself? She still watched him as she spoke.

"Are you going to return them to Ian, Mr. Fortune?"

"Not if they don't want to go."

"But you will tell him where they are."

"I'm not sure yet," I said. "Look, Mrs. Killian, I'm not the only one after them, and they may be in danger." I told her about Livingston Mall and Derry City. "I have a strong feeling they know they're in danger, know those two men I saw in Chatham."

"They're at the Hotel Lincoln Square on West Seventy-fourth Street," she said. "I don't know the room number."

I thanked her, and the black maid arrived to escort me to the front door. In the bedroom the young muscleman wasn't wearing even his jockey shorts now. Edna Killian walked into the bedroom, unbuttoning her robe.

TWENTY-THREE

ALLEGHENY DROPPED me back at La Guardia by 3:00 P.M., and I took a taxi directly to the West Side. The Lincoln Square was a cut or two above the Hotel Emerson, where I'd first found them. Some attempt had been made to keep the lobby clean and neat, the staff reasonably presentable. The desk clerk even wore a shirt and tie. He had no Campbells registered. I described them.

"Probably checked in last night," I explained.

The clerk looked me over more carefully. "That could be Mr. and Mrs. Murdoch, but I don't—"

"I should have guessed," I said, and smiled at the suspicious clerk. "He writes, Murdoch's his pen name."

I didn't want the clerk to wonder too hard about who and what I might be. He could warn them. But it didn't work.

"Very well, give me your name, I'll call up."

When someone doesn't buy one line you try another. I took out my credentials. "All right, I'm a private detective. This Alan Campbell's father hired me to find him. The old man's sick, just wants his son home. All I'm supposed to do is talk to them. If they know I'm here they might run out again.''

I backed up my sincerity with a twenty dollar bill. The hotel was classier than the Emerson downtown, but it wasn't that classy. The clerk took my twenty in his clean hands, told me the room number, and busied himself with the mail. But he didn't wink or even grin when he took the cash. Class.

I rode the elevator to the third floor. Their room number was 310. The music came to meet me. The powerful music of a full symphony orchestra and a good one. Northern music, vast and tragic, resigned to a long darkness. I recognized it as Sibelius, his Seventh and last symphony.

It wasn't music I would have connected to Alan and Helen Kay Campbell, not after meeting them. Then, if my work has taught me anything it's that there are hidden corners in all of us. Sometimes so well hidden we don't know they are there ourselves until one day they come out of our own darkness to confront us.

I knocked at the door of room 310.

The music didn't stop, but the door opened.

The big black from the stone bridge and maybe Livingston Mall held a Smith & Wesson .357 magnum and waved me inside. The gold medallion still rested on his chest hair in the ''V'' of a pale green silk shirt, and his leisure suit was white now. I stepped inside, heard him close the door behind me.

The small, pale man from the stone bridge lay on one of two twin beds. An outsize portable stereo tape machine stood on the cover beside him. The Sibelius came from its twin speakers.

A third man leaned against the door into an adjoining room. Short and thick, with braided black hair and Indian eyes, and a dark, weathered face. He sucked on a beer can like a squat baby with a bottle.

Neither Alan nor Helen Kay was in the room.

"You're pretty good," the small man on the bed said. "He's a pretty good detective, right, Dog?"

"Not so bad, J.J.," the big black said.

"You're a hard man, Dog," the small man, J.J., said. "You are a hard, mean man. You know that?"

"I calls a spade a spade, J.J.," Dog said.

J.J. smiled. On the bed he closed his eyes and moved his narrow head with the oddly round face to the music of Sibelius. His almost bloodless face was like something that never saw the sun. Flat eyes that seemed to look inward, small features and bad teeth, that mixture of young and old. No longer in the Roaring Twenties. A black jump suit now, black beret, black paratrooper boots, zippers on everything. The Special Forces on a mission. Eyes closed and listening to Sibelius.

"The end of the nineteenth century. The end of the triumph of Europe. No more rational man. No more logic and light. The end of five hundred years reaching up there for the stars. That's the Sibelius Seventh. No more Homo sapiens *über alles*, no more glory of science gonna set us all free. Gone. Finished. The end. Kaput."

The symphony faded wistfully away. The big black, Dog, yawned. The Indian at the door sucked beer.

The small man, J.J., opened his eyes. "What's Campbell want you to do with Helen Kay and the husband?"

He knew a lot more about me than I knew about them.

"Find them, call him, and hold them until he can talk to them."

"Why?"

"I suppose he wants to find out why they left home without telling him, maybe try to talk them into going home."

The small man, J.J., pressed various buttons on the portable stereo. A new music filled the hotel room. Mahler. His Third Symphony. Broad music, soaring. The outsize

stereo was clearly custom-made, special, able to change
tapes, store extra tapes, locate precise points on any tape.

"That sounds about right, don't it, Dog?" J.J. said.

"Close enough," Dog said.

"Maybe we can do business with Mr. Fortune."

"Maybe that's so, J.J.," Dog agreed.

The squat Indian sucked his can of beer and leaned
against the closed door into the next room as if he were
asleep standing up. The warrior in enemy country, snatch-
ing sleep. Dog yawned again, spun the cylinder on his .357
magnum to check the chambers. J.J. listened to Mahler.

"Over, the nineteenth century," the small man said to the
ceiling of the hotel room. "Sibelius, he knew. That Seventh is the good-bye, so long to five hundred years of big
plans. From now on we'd all live in a different world, a different time. A new ball game, and you hear it in Mahler."
He lay on the bed and heard it in Mahler. "A world where
we ain't so glorious, and we got no way to get to the stars.
A new kind of ball game. Maybe smaller, maybe bigger,
maybe just so damned different we can't even think about
it. We don't know what it's gonna be, but we know nothin's gonna be the same again." He talked to no one in particular and to everyone. Moved in and out of the music and
his own mind. "You ever think about your arm, Fortune?"

"I think about it."

"You think about where it is right now?"

"Sometimes. Sometimes I wonder if the arm thinks about
me."

He turned his head on the bed to look at me again. The
flat eyes immobile under blow-dried hair that made him
look like the caricature of some teenage TV idol. Then he
looked back at the ceiling, pressed more buttons on the expensive portable. He knew the exact part of the music he

wanted, the exact tape, and the special machine had the electronics to find it.

"Death, that's Mahler. Everything's death. Only he don't scream about it, just sad we all got born so we could die." A horn call took over the music. A distant horn call, alone in the mountains. "The twentieth century, that's Mahler. The Nazis and Stalin. Vietnam and the Gulag. Nixon and Churchill. Masturbate on the goddamn couch and watch football on the TV. Last year we all went to Acapulco, where'll we all go this year? Get on the bandwagon. Follow the dictator. Bash babies against walls or maybe we lose what we got. It's too fucking cold up ahead, too fucking dark."

His speech was that mixture of big words, bad grammar, and street language that is a mark of the half-educated, the school dropout who reads too much in thick books. A man who talked to himself, moved in and out of time, his eyes turned inward.

"We got them, Fortune. We sell them back to Campbell for a cool million. We don't get the bucks, Dog blows 'em both away."

"No dough, they go," Dog said.

The deep voice of a mezzo sang in the room. A song of a dark morning and a distant day. "There was this guy used to see the sun come up every mornin' on the train going to work. After a while he figured out he saw it in the same place on the same day every year. He started to figure the place for each day until he got so he could look at where the sun come up and tell you exactly what day it was, what month, what time. He did that for twenty-five years. It made him feel real good. Every day he rode that same train and saw the sun come up the same exact place every damned day of every damned year."

It was as if he thought about whatever happened to rise into his mind, whatever came to his mind on the music or

probably anything else, and then said it aloud to anyone or
no one. Unconcerned whether anyone wanted to hear it or
not. Unconcerned with anything except what he was thinking. "You ever think about losing the other arm?"

"Sometimes," I said.

"All the time," he said. "You don't ever forget." He listened to the dark mezzo song of Mahler, to the deep pain of
the dark song. "Animals, they live to stay alive. With animals life is just staying alive day to day. We solved that
problem. Most of us know we're gonna be alive tomorrow,
so what do we live for? To play cards in some lousy hotel
room? Drink beer? Make a million? Ride a dirt bike all over
and going no place? You ever wonder about that, Fortune?"

"I wonder," I said. "I wonder about a lot of things. For
instance, I wonder why a fast-food operator in Livingston
and a landlady in Derry City are dead? I wonder where they
fit into all this?"

Sometimes you have to take a chance. You don't want to,
you wish you didn't have to, but sometimes you have to
forget the risk, try not to think of what could happen to you.
You have to know.

"I wouldn't know," J.J. said. "You know anything about
those folks, Dog?"

The big black in the white leisure suit stuffed the .357
magnum away in some clever holster under his white vest.
"Can't say I do, J.J."

There was a casualness to it all that made me cold. A
matter of business. All calm and reasonable. A simple deal
from a different world. An alien world. A world of their
own where they lived by their own rules.

"One million," J.J. said. "Campbell gets his chicks."

The massive finale of the Mahler Third rose in sweeping
hammer blows to a final hope and despair. Dog looked at
his watch. The Indian walked from his door into the bath-

room and returned with a fresh can of beer. J.J. watched the
Indian to the bathroom and back again. I watched J.J.

"I'm not sure Campbell can raise that kind of cash," I
said, "and I'm not sure Alan's worth that much to him."

J.J. punched buttons on the big stereo. Sibelius again, the
Seventh Symphony once more. J.J. listened on the bed.

"Name a ball-park number," he said.

"A quarter of a million."

"Half."

"If you want complications. My guess is that a quarter of
a million is the best he could do on his own now."

J.J. listened to his Sibelius. "Dog?"

The big black considered me, and shrugged. The Indian
made a low noise.

"Looks like we're all reasonable," J.J. said. "Two
hundred and fifty big ones then."

"How does he know you really have them?"

"We call him." He closed his eyes and went on listening
to his music. "Two hundred and fifty big ones or Lassie
don't come home, no happy fade-out. The dam breaks and
no rescue. The Lone Ranger don't ride."

"Can we call you in this hotel?"

He opened his eyes. "You don't call us nowhere." He
closed his eyes again. "Dog!"

I felt the point of a sharp, thin knife against my back. Dog
moved like a shadow. I walked from the room with the Sibelius following me. We rode down in the elevator. Dog
smiled to the desk clerk as we went by. I smiled too. On the
street the knife prodded me toward Amsterdam Avenue.

"Take a cab. Go all the way down to that office you got."

I waved for a taxi. When one came I got in and told the
driver to take me down to my office. I didn't look behind
me. I sat back and rode quietly south on Amsterdam. Until
we reached Sixty-fifth Street.

"Turn left. Then back uptown on Broadway."

I paid the taxi off on the corner of Seventy-second, walked back up to Seventy-fourth. I surveyed the block cautiously before I walked ahead on the opposite side of the street from the Hotel Lincoln Square. J.J., Dog, and the Indian were no amateurs. They could have left someone staked out to be sure I didn't try to do what I was trying to do. Or they could have skipped the instant Dog walked me out and sent me south.

Those were the risks I had to take. If they'd already gone, I would waste a lot of time and lose their trail entirely. If they were staked out and spotted me, I might not have any time left to waste.

From a convenient doorway I watched the hotel. Waited, sweating despite the sharp wind blowing up from the river.

TWENTY-FOUR

IT GREW DARK. The wind from the river grew colder. I waited, huddled in my old duffel coat, my lone hand deep in the pocket, while the wind scoured the doorway and I hoped at least it wouldn't snow.

An hour, and they all came out together. The small man, J.J., Dog, the Indian, and Alan and Helen Kay Campbell. I'd never really had much hope that they didn't have them. In front of the hotel they all stood bunched together in the wind. There was something odd about the way they stood there waiting in front of the hotel like a group of tourists looking for their tour bus. I didn't have time to think about what it was. I realized that they had to be waiting for the gaudy red Lincoln limousine. It meant I needed wheels to follow, and that there was a fourth member of the gang. At least. Luckily, Seventy-fourth went east. I slipped quickly up to Broadway, found a cruising cab.

"Wait right here."

"It's your money," the driver said.

The red limo came out of Seventy-fourth and turned south on Broadway. It looked like a rolling ruby in the midst of lumps of coal. A hell of a vehicle for a kidnapping. That feeling of oddness again. Or maybe J.J. and his minions didn't give a damn, liked to flaunt danger.

"Follow that red limo," I said.

"You're kidding," the cabbie said.

"Never mind the comedy. Just don't lose them."

"Mister—"

"There'll be a big tip."

"How big?"

"Double the fare."

"So we follow that limo."

The big red car was moving away down Broadway. We tailed through the heavy night traffic to Sixty-fifth and across town to Central Park West. The limousine crossed the park at Sixty-sixth Street and went through the East Side to Second Avenue and all the way down to the Midtown Tunnel.

"Hey, I didn't figure on no tunnel trip," the driver said.

"If we go too far I'll double the return fare."

"You got class." I could see his face in the rearview mirror looking up at it to watch me. "Private eye?"

"Naturally."

"Sure," he agreed as we emerged from the tunnel into Queens. "You do this kind of thing much?"

"You want to be my cab on call?"

"Why not?"

He liked quadruple fares, especially since he would only have to kick in to the company what was on the meter. The big red Lincoln cruised along the Long Island Expressway until it finally turned into the Van Wyck and headed straight south. I knew now where we were going. So did the cab driver.

"Got to be Kennedy. That's double fare already, right?"

"You've got the double doubled."

"I like class." He continued to watch me in his mirror. "It pays good? This private eye stuff?"

"If I'm lucky I'll get my money back. Stick to hacking."

"It don't pay what it used to, mister."

"Nothing pays what it used to."

"'Cept for the big companies. They gets paid better every year, makes bigger profits."

"You're an enemy of free enterprise?"

"Hey, not me. I figures on gettin' up there with the winners, right?"

"That's how it's done," I said.

The red limousine reached Kennedy and drove around to the American Airlines terminal area. I paid the cabbie half the doubled fare, and told him to wait for me. I followed the five of them to the main ticket area. Whoever their driver was he remained with the big red limousine. They all checked in at a ticket counter. Dog handled the details while the others stood in a small group. Their baggage gone, including the backpacks of Alan and Helen Kay, they all trooped to an examination station, went through, and on toward the lounge and cafeteria area.

They had passed through the detectors without a hitch! All of them. Who had the weapons? If they had no weapons, what was keeping Alan and Helen Kay from escaping? Did J.J., Dog, or the Indian have some kind of weapon that didn't show on a metal detector? Or did they have a weapon that wasn't physical at all, some hold as strong as any threat of violence?

They went into the cafeteria. Dog and the Indian got on the food line, Helen Kay and Alan sat with J.J. at a table. Alan seemed to watch the dark runways through the windows. Helen Kay watched J.J., her face sullen under her short hair. J.J. watched a couple at the table next to them.

An older couple. A round little man with a white tonsure of hair and a mild face, who wore a heavy gray sweater under his dark blue suit. An imposing woman with a firm manner and an expensive gray wool dress. She had a full bosom like a breastplate, looked at her watch impatiently.

A young man who looked like a replica of the old man fifty years ago carried a full tray to the older couple's table. He began to set plates and cups on the table. There were three cups of coffee.

"Really, Maxwell!" the old woman said. "I told you to bring milk for your grandfather. Coffee upsets him."

The old man said, "One cup won't hurt me, Phyllis."

"Any cup upsets your nerves and your stomach, makes you impossible. Take it back, Maxwell. Bring him milk."

The young man glanced at his grandfather. The old man said nothing. It's not a matter of sex or gender. Some people are rulers and some are ruled, some are winners and some losers. It has to do with sensitivity. The sensitive, the vulnerable, will always lose.

J.J. got up and stood over the old couple's table. Menacing in his black combat outfit like a storm trooper, the gestapo.

"You want coffee, mister, you take coffee."

The old man blinked. "I really don't—"

"Just what business is it of yours!" the woman demanded.

"Shut up!" J.J. said, not looking at the woman. Looking only at the man as heads turned all through the cafeteria. "You take what you want. You don't let her tell you what to do."

"Manager!" the woman cried. "Maxwell, call the police!"

J.J. watched the old man. "Drink your coffee."

The old man picked up the cup, drank. He drank it all. He even smiled. Just a little.

"You want coffee, you drink coffee," J.J. said.

Two airport policemen strode into the cafeteria and up to the table. Dog and the Indian stood behind J.J. and watched the airport cops. For a moment the five faced each other. The whole restaurant watched the confrontation.

"Arrest them!" the old woman said.

J.J. smiled. "We're just leaving, officers."

"Okay," one of the policemen said. "You do that."

"Sorry and all that," J.J. said.

"Just move on and don't bother other people," the second officer said.

Everyone watched the confrontation. Except me. I watched Alan Campbell and Helen Kay. They sat alone at the table behind J.J., Dog, and the Indian. Not ten feet from the two airport policemen. They sat and watched. Close to the police, all three of their kidnappers looking the other way, they sat and made no attempt to escape. What hold did J.J., Dog, and the Indian have on them? What kind of kidnapping was it? What kind of kidnappers use a red limousine, stand in a cozy group with their victims to wait for a car and ticket confirmation? What kidnappers take their captives on a commercial airline flight? What victims walk meekly through a crowded airport with no move to escape?

"Just move on," the airport cop said.

J.J. laughed, and they went back to their table and then left the cafeteria with Alan and Helen Kay. They went on into the waiting room. I circled to come in at the other side. A direct flight to Phoenix, Arizona, was being announced for immediate boarding. When I reached the other entrance they were already going into the boarding tunnel—Alan and Helen Kay, the Indian, Dog bringing up the rear. I didn't see J.J. Had he gone on first, before I reached the entrance, or had he gone somewhere else? Spotted me and doubled back?

I hurried back the way I'd come, looking for him. I didn't see him. The two airport policemen were still standing outside the cafeteria acting unconcerned. I circled the entire waiting area. The gates were closed on the Phoenix flight. I went back along the passage to the terminal and the parking lots, reached my waiting taxi without seeing J.J. The red limousine was gone.

"When did it leave?"

"Couple or five minutes ago," the cabbie said.

"Did anyone come out of the terminal and get in it?"

"Didn't see anyone get in it. You ready to go back?"

It was a long drive back into the city, I had time to think. If I hadn't just missed J.J. getting on the plane first, why had he stayed behind alone? They had taken a direct flight to Phoenix, Arizona. Flagstaff, Helen Kay Campbell's hometown, was just over a hundred miles north of Phoenix.

At my apartment I had to get the cash to pay the driver from my desk. Then I called Ian Campbell.

I got a recording with Campbell's cool voice instructing me to leave my name and message after the beep. I left my name and my message—call me, urgent. I didn't want him to get the call from J.J. or Dog before I told him.

TWENTY-FIVE

TWO HOURS OF dozing. It was better than television, and to hell with Ian Campbell. No one could do anything until the kidnappers called anyway. I called Kay Michaels.

"Yes?"

How long was it since I'd heard her low voice. Sensed her almost-green eyes and easy smile at the other end of the line. Six months, give or take, and it had been nice in California.

"Dan," I said. "You're a hard woman to reach."

"You reached me six months ago. I'm just hard to find at home when I get back to New York," her low voice said. "How are you, Dan?"

"At the moment frustrated. Also tired and tied down. Maybe I shouldn't have called. Wasting your New York time."

"I'm glad you called. When I'm here I wait for the ring."

"At least I wanted to hear your voice."

"At least that. Until when, Dan?"

"Tomorrow night?"

It was easy to say to hell with Ian Campbell, but I knew I couldn't make it stick. I had to try to reach him tonight. At least try. She didn't push me.

"I've got tickets for the big musical at The Imperial," she said.

It was a musical adaptation of *Finnegans Wake*. A hundred dollars a ticket and the show lasted eight hours. An event. The only way to a popular success these days. For any real success, it had to be an EVENT! The art form of the end of the twentieth century. Trumpets summoning the hordes to the mass ritual. Not the substance, only the shadow. Capering mute and enormous on a giant screen.

"Throw them away," I said. "I can't keep your clothes on for eight hours."

"We'll meet early," she said. "Anyway, there's a dinner break, and who needs food? Then afterward we can—"

"Okay! Paint me no more possibilities tonight. Are you staying alone where you are?"

"I'll make sure I am tomorrow."

"Eat a big lunch."

"No. I want to be ravenous when you arrive."

"Jesus," I said. "I have to wait for a call here or..." I breathed hard in my silent loft. "Miss me?"

"For six months. I can wait one more day."

"I can't," I said.

"Yes you can."

"I can," I said. "Isn't that sad."

"I'll wait for your call," she said, "get some rest for tomorrow."

One of the ways you tell that it is real is when you hang up you smile. You smile even when you're not going to see her that day. I smiled in the silent loft room with only the late-night street sounds of New York somewhere outside. Until 2:00 A.M., and then I called Chatham again. I got the same recording and left the same message. There was no way I could tell Campbell over a recording machine that his son had been kidnapped. At 3:30 A.M. I gave up.

Where was Ian Campbell at almost four in the morning?

TWENTY-SIX

CAMPBELL'S REDHEADED secretary still stared at my missing arm. Campbell was in his office.

"But he can't be disturbed," the secretary said. She liked that part of her work, turning people down.

"It's urgent," I said. "It's so urgent it was urgent yesterday."

"You can wait in Mr. Aherne's office. They're both in Mr. Campbell's office."

I couldn't tell her about the kidnapping before I told Ian Campbell. That limited my impressiveness. I went into Aherne's office on the other side of the connecting secretarial area.

"It's been necessary for a long time, Max."

I glanced all around Aherne's office. I was alone.

"Tell me about it."

Aherne's voice. But where from?

"There's no sense getting belligerent, Max."

The other voice was Ian Campbell, I was sure of that. They were talking in Campbell's office on the opposite side of the secretarial room. And I was hearing them. From an air duct? Thin walls? Some quirk of acoustics from one open window to another?

"What is there sense in getting, old partner?" Aherne's voice said. It was a long way from friendly.

"There's no sense getting nasty either. I think we can do this and remain friends, maybe work together in the future. You know me, Max."

"Bullshit! You want it as nasty as you can make it. You need your fun, your kicks! I know you all right. We won't work together in the future, and we never were friends!"

From the intercom. I leaned closer to it where it stood on Aherne's desk. The key to the secretary's unit was open. So out in her connecting office the redhead was listening in somehow, and it was all being passed on along the line to Aherne's office.

"Okay, Max, we'll play it hard-nosed. I have plans for the company and you don't fit into them. There are things I want to do, with the company and outside the company, and I don't want you around. Take your share payout and go somewhere else. Start a new company, that's what you're good at. When a company's small you're valuable, but beyond a certain point of growth you're a liability."

"I'll fight you, Ian. All the way."

There was a long, steady grinding sound as if Campbell were swinging slowly from side to side in his desk chair. A slow, intense swinging that seemed to radiate not nerves but excitement. A pleasure in it, as Aherne had said, kicks.

"We've always wanted different things, Max. I knew that from the start, if you didn't. For ourselves and for the company. It's time for the company to go in my direction."

"What direction is that?"

"That won't be any of your business now. You wouldn't like the direction, wouldn't know what to do. It's time for a younger staff, full professionals, to run the day-to-day operations, and there's only room for one chief when that happens."

In a silence from Campbell's office there was only the metallic grinding of his constantly swiveling desk chair.

"You decided all that all by yourself?" Aherne's voice said.

The silence and metallic grinding of the swinging desk chair was joined by the creak of another chair. Like the left-hand accompaniment to Campbell's swivel chair. I could see that office in my mind. The creaking had to be from one of the polished cane chairs that faced Campbell's desk. They sat facing each other across the huge inlaid desk, Campbell swinging from side to side in his desk chair, Aherne rhythmically teetering the straight cane chair on its back legs.

"All by myself, Max."

"And I'm just going to smile and let you do it."

"Seventy-thirty says you can't stop me."

The cane chair creaked louder.

"I salute and march away like a good boy."

The grinding of the metal springs of the desk chair went steadily on.

"You march away. I don't give a damn what else you do."

I could see them as clearly as if I were standing in that office across the secretarial area. Facing each other over the inlaid desk in what would have been total silence except for the grinding of the desk chair and the creak of the cane chair. Max Aherne with contempt in his eyes. Ian Campbell smiling. Only a faint smile, but a smile.

"Okay, it's in the open now," Max Aherne's voice said. *"It's been there a long time, but now we know. We can go on from here. You can't force me out, no matter what you say. You can only buy me out, and I won't sell."*

"Yes," Campbell said, *"You'll sell."*

"No," Aherne said.

"If you don't sell me your share at a reasonable price I'll fix it so that the company makes no profit at all. Not ever. I'll fire you, and that I can do. You'll have no salary, no profits, no income. You'll own thirty percent of nothing."

I imagined Campbell's smile widening. Yet when Aherne's voice came again it was calm and quiet, without anger. As if a storm had passed. The calm of a man who knows the battle is over. Won or lost, it was over.

"So now you've got it. I should have seen it, shouldn't I? All the new vice-presidents. The old people gone. I'm almost the last one who can call you Ian, right? The last one you have to explain anything to."

The metallic grinding of Campbell's desk chair ceased, and when his voice came over the intercom it was as if he hadn't been in the room while Aherne had been talking, as if Aherne had said nothing.

"You'll get a fair payout. You can set up on your own."

"What do you want to do I wouldn't agree with, Ian?"

"Maybe a little more than fair."

"What do you want to hide?"

The swivel chair gave a loud rasp. I heard Campbell's footsteps on the carpet. His voice came from somewhere across the room distant from his desk and intercom.

"Look at them down there. Going nowhere. Nowhere at all. Doing just what they're told to do and going nowhere."

I realized he was standing at one of his windows looking down at the company parking lot and the street beyond.

"Now no one can tell me to do anything. Now I'm going somewhere."

There was a strange sound from the unseen office. Odd and muffled. Ian Campbell was laughing. Across the office at his window, looking down on the people and laughing.

"I think I'll go into politics. I'm good-looking enough, have my hair, look younger than I am. I've got friends with money and friends who know how to raise money. The way I'm going to operate the company I'll have plenty of time— let the vice-presidents run the show and fight each other to see who I'll finally make president. Politics is fun and good for business. State office, then go for Congress. Why not? I'm successful, have the right education and connections."

Aherne's voice was almost a sneer. *"Successful? What the hell have you done? If the company went out of business tomorrow who would miss us? We don't make anything really necessary, just convenience software. A hundred companies could do what we do. We get people to buy what we make by hard promotion and selling. Not one thing important would be different if we'd never started."*

The swivel chair rasped, Campbell's voice was back at his desk. *"I'm sorry you feel that bitter, Max. You just don't fit here anymore."*

Now Aherne stood up, the straight chair creaked. *"How do we get it settled?"*

"My lawyer will handle the details."

"You better take me off the company Christmas list."

"You'll probably still be here at Christmas."

"But not next year. No sense wasting a basket of cheese and salami on someone who won't be around next year."

Ian Campbell was silent in the unseen office. I sensed Max Aherne standing there and watching Campbell. Aherne laughed.

"By God, I'll bet you do take me off the Christmas list! You've got no class, Ian. No class at all."

Campbell's voice was thin. *"You'll get your damned cheese."*

"You know, Ian, I think you miss the point."

"The point of what?"

"Of everything."

I heard the fading footsteps on the office carpet and the opening of a door. A moment later Max Aherne came into his own office. He looked at me where I sat on the edge of his desk. He looked at the still-open intercom.

"Can he do it?" I asked.

We could both hear Ian Campbell still swinging back and forth in his swivel chair.

"He can," Aherne said. "He will. What I wonder about is why? I mean, the real reason."

"What do you think it could be?"

Aherne shrugged. "Whatever it is, the hell with it. I need a drink."

He opened his briefcase, put all the papers from his desk into it, and walked out.

TWENTY-SEVEN

IAN CAMPBELL was at his window again when the red-headed secretary ushered me in. He was staring out and down at the parking lot, at the people walking in and out of his plant and passing on the street beyond. Or maybe he was watching something more definite. Such as Max Aherne driving away.

"How long have you been planning to squeeze Aherne out?"

He didn't turn or even move. "I told you before to stay out of my business affairs."

"I try," I said, "but it's hard. Where were you last night until four A.M. or later?"

His back remained toward me. He still didn't move there at the window. "With my controller and my lawyer. I had to be sure I had Aherne cold." Now he turned. Sharply. "You were trying to reach me?"

"I left a message on your machine."

He waved that away. "It got so late I slept here on the couch. You found Alan?"

"Sit down," I said.

"Where is he? Take me, right now!"

"I found them," I said, "and I lost them. You'd better sit down."

"I don't want to sit down! Tell me!"

His eyes never looked away from my face as I told him how I had found them at the Hotel Emerson, and lost them. How I'd tracked them to the Hotel Lincoln Square, and about J.J., Dog, the Indian, the fourth man and the kidnapping. It didn't make me sound too good, but Campbell had other things on his mind.

"No police," he said. "You hear? No police, no FBI."

He went on watching me, and that was what he said. Before anything else. Then he turned away again to look out the window. Out and down at the people in his parking lot and passing on the Chatham street. No police, no FBI, and his back to me. "You were told to call me. Find them and call me first! Before you did anything else. Before you talked to them. Before you goddamn lost them!"

"I found them, they didn't want to come back to Chatham, I had to talk to them."

No police, no FBI. He came away from the window. "You didn't call me, you lost them, you let a bunch of weirdos kidnap them! What the hell am I paying you for?"

"I'm not sure," I said. "What are you paying me for? What am I really doing?"

"I'm not paying you to forget to call me when you find them! I'm not paying you to lose them! I'm not paying you to let them be kidnapped without doing a damn thing!"

"What should I have done, Campbell? Jumped up and down? Stamped my foot? Warned those kidnappers that they were committing a serious crime?"

He sat down in his desk chair and began his swiveling. "Goddamn it, Fortune, if you'd called me when you found them the first time, none of this would have happened! They might be back here by now!"

"I think all of it would have happened just as it did." I was still standing. "They don't want to talk to you. They didn't want to be found. Not by me, not by you, not by anyone from Chatham."

He sat silent behind his inlaid desk, swiveling back and forth with that slow, steady swiveling the way other men doodle or play with the pencils on their desks. "Who are they, Fortune? What do they want with Alan?"

No police and no FBI. Before he said anything else.

"I thought maybe you could tell me," I said.

"Me?" He even stopped swiveling for a moment. "What are you talking about? What would I know about a gang of professional gunmen? Gangsters!"

"You're sure they're not part of the something I've been told to stay out of?" I said. "Your business or your private life?"

He swiveled again. "What gives you that idea?"

"When I got back to the hotel room at the Emerson after Alan and Helen Kay had suckered me, your lady friend was in the room. Seems she's out looking for Alan and Helen Kay too. How come?"

"My lady friend?"

"Leah Aherne."

Campbell stopped the swiveling once more. "Leah was at that hotel? In New York? Looking for Alan?"

"That's what I think I just said."

Again the swiveling. "What the hell for?"

"To help you out. That's what she said anyway. She thinks you're worried about more than Alan. She's worried that you're worried. Are you worried, Campbell? About more than Alan?"

"Everybody's worried about something," he said. "I didn't ask her to help me. With Alan or anything else."

"Does she know about you and her father? The cute little squeeze you're putting on Aherne?"

"I don't see how."

"And you know nothing about the kidnappers?"

"Not a goddamned thing!" The swiveling became more violent, and so did his voice. "I didn't hire you to interrogate me, Fortune, and I didn't hire you to let Alan be kidnapped!"

"I didn't let him be kidnapped," I said. "But I'm not so sure somebody didn't let him get kidnapped."

Now he forgot about his swiveling. "What? What do you mean? Who let him be kidnapped?"

"Maybe himself."

"Alan?"

"Or Helen Kay, or someone damned close to them."

"What in hell are you talking about?"

"There's something awful peculiar about this kidnapping, Campbell." I sat down now. On one of the creaking wicker chairs that faced Campbell's desk, and told him about the five of them standing in front of the Hotel Lincoln Square waiting for the red Lincoln, about Alan and Helen Kay waiting quietly with J.J. and the Indian while Dog checked in. I described all five of them trooping through the detector station, and the big argument scene in the cafeteria when Alan and Helen Kay had been momentarily forgotten by their captors. "Okay, the gang could have had some kind of weapon the detectors didn't pick up, but

Alan and Helen Kay had a chance to make a run in that cafeteria and they didn't. Why? What kind of kidnapping is it? What hold do the kidnappers have on them I don't know about?''

Campbell sat back and closed his eyes. Neither swiveling nor looking at me he rubbed slowly at his closed eyes with both hands. "Perhaps they were just afraid to try, Fortune. Perhaps they were afraid too many bystanders would be hurt."

"Maybe, only I never heard of a kidnap victim who thinks about a damn thing except getting away, and who ever heard of kidnappers taking the victim on a commercial flight? Surrounded by people, flight personnel, attendants, guards. No, J.J. and his gang knew Alan and Helen Kay wouldn't try to get away. Why?"

Campbell had no answer in the quiet office. At least, not for me. He sat there rubbing at his closed eyes as we both listened to the cars down in the parking lot and the voices of the secretaries out in the office between his and Aherne's. It was lunchtime.

"Where did they take them, Fortune?"

"The jet was nonstop to Phoenix." I didn't mention that I wasn't at all sure J.J. had been on the jet.

"Arizona?"

"Where Helen Kay comes from," I said. "Flagstaff isn't much more than a hundred miles north of Phoenix."

"You think they're from Arizona? The kidnappers? They've taken Alan and Helen Kay to Arizona?"

"That's how it looks. I can go out and try to pick them up. Flagstaff's a small city."

Now he was up. "You won't go anywhere near Arizona! Not until I've been contacted, you understand? Not until those gunmen tell us to go to Arizona."

"They'll tell you to get two hundred and fifty thousand dollars in small bills."

"Then I'll get it, and then we'll go to Arizona, if that's where they tell us to go."

I stood up. "Maybe you won't hear from them. Maybe they won't ask for money. I don't know what yet, but there's something wrong about this kidnapping."

He watched me. "All right, go on investigating but be careful. You lost Alan twice, Fortune, don't get him killed. Not if you want to see any money out of this job."

He was a sweet client. Almost as good a client as he was a partner. He was also not a man I'd have expected to just hand over a quarter of a million dollars, even for a son. Not without a lot more fight.

TWENTY-EIGHT

It was 2:00 P.M. before I got back to New York, the November afternoon gray with a low sky that threatened snow and a wind blowing river to river that would turn it into a blizzard. I tucked my neck down inside my old duffel coat and looked for a cab on the corner of Ninth Street and Sixth Avenue. Sarah Borden came from Flagstaff. She seemed like a good place to start finding out what, if anything, was wrong about the kidnapping.

The taxi dropped me in front of 517 Perry. On the gray day there was light in the upper-floor windows of the four-story Georgian brownstone, but Sarah Borden's ground-floor apartment was dark. Her mail was still in the vestibule box, and no one answered my rings. At two-thirty in the afternoon an actress could be anywhere, and I didn't know who her agent was. It had already begun to snow.

I cabbed it back up to my office, the cabbie cursing the snow all the way, swearing that after he dropped me he was pulling off the streets, yessir. No damn way he was gonna

stay on the goddamn streets in no snow. In my office I called
my answering service. They had another message from Kay
Michaels. She didn't want to wait until five. She was alone
now in her friend's apartment. In case I'd forgotten to write
it down she gave her address again—in the east eighties, 2C.

I could go back to the Hotel Lincoln Square to see if J.J.,
Dog, and the Indian had left any leads behind, but even in
a semifleabag they clean out the rooms fast for the next
tenant and to see if anything has been forgotten they can
pocket. I should try to find out where they'd been staying in
town, where they had garaged the Lincoln. Maybe J.J. had
even returned to wherever they had been staying.

And I wanted to talk to Leah Aherne again.

But it all sounded like long, slow work.

From my desk chair I watched the snow falling over the
city outside my windows. Thick and silent, muting the noise
of men and machines, covering the gaudiness and the dirt,
softening the harshness of stone and indifference. A long
time ago, even before I lost my arm, I fell in love with a girl
from uptown. She was small, excited and exciting, lived in
a penthouse on Central Park South, and dazzled the boy
from Chelsea. We walked hand-in-hand along the busy,
alive midtown streets and through the winter park, and we
sat warm in her penthouse behind the high windows and
watched the snow fall all across the city and the park. There
was a grand piano in that penthouse, and she played Cho-
pin—the Etude opus 10 no. 3. It became our music, and,
ever since, snow falling outside the dark windows has made
me think of the warmth of a woman behind those windows
out of the falling snow.

I got my beret and duffel coat and went out. Leah Aherne
could wait until tomorrow. I found a solitary cab outside the
Chelsea Hotel and rode up to the east eighties and apartment 2C. Tomorrow I would work again for Ian Campbell.
I rang the bell of 2C. No one answered. I looked at the door.

t was slightly ajar, unlocked, and not quite closed. I went
nside.

She was in the bedroom. In the bed. Under the covers and
waiting for me. She is a tall woman, long under the covers,
and all I could see in the dim bedroom was her black hair
and almost-green eyes and easy smile. Long black hair that
framed alert eyes. Waiting eyes, darker in the reflected light
of the falling snow outside, the smile not as easy as when I
had first come into the bedroom.

I undressed out of my mound of snow clothes and
touched her high breasts as her long legs raised to meet me.
Lean and tall and soft and warm and tight and curled under and in and around me all at the same time.

After, we lay quiet under the covers and watched the
now. She smoked and I held her. A one-armed man has to
make choices. I couldn't smoke and hold her at the same
time. I held her. She is thirty-five, Kay Michaels, old for a
model, young for me. In the bed we listened to the faint
rushing of the snow against the walls of the city, a moving
shadow of silence outside the windows, and talked about
what people talk about after making love. About our lives.

"I'm glad I came east." She smoked, the room blue-white
with the reflection of the snow. "I wasn't until tonight.
Nobody wants me as an actress. Hey, you're a model, kid!
You're a big model, a big success, rich, enjoy it."

She was a successful model; she made a lot of money. She
was pleased with that, yes. She liked being a successful
model. Yet it wasn't what she really wanted to do, and the
victory was limited, the triumph questionable.

"Maybe I ask too much, Dan. I haven't done what I
wanted to do, gotten near what I dreamed about. But I guess
I haven't had to do as much of what I didn't want to do as
most people, and maybe I've gotten more of what I dreamed
about than most. Is that maybe a successful life? Not having to do much of what you don't want to do?"

"Why not," I said. The snow still fell outside the win
dows. "Everyone settles for less."

"What did you settle for?"

"Making an easy living."

"I don't believe that."

Her breasts moved against me, small and high. She kissed
me. We were in a cave, safe and warm, hidden by the snow

I said, "I knew a man who played in a regular poker game
and lost most of the time. Not much, but a little almost
every time. He began to feel like a fool playing regularly and
losing most of the time. He wondered if he was a pigeon, a
sucker. He talked of quitting. But he loved the game, en
joyed it almost more than anything. Then he found an an
swer. He decided that he simply didn't take the game as
seriously as two of the players. He wasn't as disciplined as
a third. That meant he would always be the fourth best
player in the game no matter how well he played. He would
always be, over the year, among the losers, if the smallest
loser. When he worked that out he was happy. It gave him
the justification he needed to lose and still go on playing. He
knew why he lost, he knew the truth, therefore he wasn't a
sucker. As long as he knew, understood, it didn't matter if
he won or lost."

She put out her cigarette, snuggled closer, her naked back
to the windows and the silent snow. "I was never status
conscious. That's not good in a status-oriented society like
ours. No one wants to know what you can do, only what
your label, your title, says you can do. The title counts, not
the ability. Who said, 'Take the cash and let the credit go'?
Not in our world. Today you'd better learn to get the credit
when you're young even if you have to work for nothing
More credit today, more cash tomorrow. I've got talent as
an actress, but status as a model, and a model I'll stay."

She talked in the dark room softened by the blue white light of the snow and moved against me as softly as the snow, sensual.

I said, "I'm on this rabbit case that's turned into a kidnapping." I told her everything I'd done, summarized all I knew. For her or for me? "There's something damned peculiar about the kidnapping, and I think Ian Campbell is after something more than getting his son to come home. If it were only his son he'd fight harder. He'd let the police and the FBI work on it. He's a smart man, he knows that's the best way. But he has to try to handle it alone, get to Alan first."

She listened, took my lone hand where it held her naked against me. She squeezed my hand.

"I want you to stay," she said.

"I want to stay."

"All night."

"At least," I said.

And I had tried. I wanted to forget about Ian Campbell and his problems. Forget, at least for one night in the warmth out of the snow, about J.J., Dog, and the Indian wherever they were. Not think of Sarah Borden or Leah Aherne. But I couldn't do it. It was there, waiting, and even Kay Michaels couldn't make it go away, warm away the restless need to know, to work, to push on along the road to the end. The affliction of the end of the twentieth century, the inability to relax, to rest, to float like the falling snow.

"I want you to stay all night," Kay Michaels said, "but I understand."

"I don't," I said. I got up. "Tomorrow."

"Tomorrow."

I dressed again in my mound of clothes retrieved from the floor of the dark room where she lay silent and alone in the warmth of the bed and went out into the snow. I asked myself no questions. The answers, at this moment as I trudged through the snow toward Lexington Avenue, would make no difference. On Lexington I found a solitary cruising taxi braving the snow. A snow that was already slackening, turning wet, as I rode down to my office to get Leah Aherne's address. A silent ride, the driver an isolated man out in the snow only for the money.

The distant ringing of my telephone reached me as I opened the street door. A distinct ring, clear down the empty stairwell of the night building, carrying out into the streets silent with the drifts of snow. It stopped, answered by the answering service. And started again as I reached my third-floor door. I opened the door, turned on the light, and the ringing stopped. I waited a moment, called the answering service. They had no messages.

Either two people had called at almost the same time and left no message, or someone badly wanted to reach me and only me. I sat down at the desk without taking off my duffel coat and waited. It was a short wait. On the second ring, I picked up the receiver.

"Fortune? I've been calling you for an hour!" Steve Norris, his voice anxious, even scared. "It's Sarah Borden. There's a light in her apartment, and her phone's busy, but she doesn't answer her door!"

"You've been seeing Sarah Borden?"

"No. I mean, yes and no. I saw her for a late drink the night we met her, but I haven't since. Tonight I—"

"You've been trying to see her?"

"Yes, I've been trying to see her!" Nervous and on edge. "She told me to call tonight, said we could get together for a late dinner. I've been calling since seven o'clock and her line's been busy the whole time. About nine I decided to come down to her apartment so I'd be here when she hung up. But the line's still busy and there's light in her apartment and she still doesn't answer the door! She—"

"Where are you now?"

"In a bar around the corner from Perry Street."

"I'll come down."

I hung up and went back out again. It sounded as if Norris had been chasing Sarah Borden ever since I'd last seen him two nights ago. A little sexual adventure, or something else? I thought about it as I looked for another taxi in the thinning snow that was turning to sleet. In another few hours the city would be a disaster of ice and slush, and this time I had no luck with a taxi. I went down into the subway.

TWENTY-NINE

THE COLD SLEET drove into my face as I walked from Sheridan Square to Perry Street. There was light now in the windows of the ground floor of number 517. Far to the rear behind the drawn shades of the front windows. Norris stepped out of a dark doorway across the street.

"Her phone's still busy, Fortune."

I stood in front of the old Georgian brownstone and listened. There were no sounds inside the apartment in the snow-silenced city. I heard no voice talking on the telephone.

"She could be all the way in the back," I said, "talking low."

Norris wore a proper three-piece suit and looked frozen, as if he'd been silently watching Sarah Borden's apartment for some time, his dark, curly hair with the silvered temples wet and blown ragged. A dark blue pin-striped suit this time. White shirt, silk foulard tie, the dashing tasseled half boots. An executive on the town, but his handsome face was drawn, the stubborn jaw uncertain. His football player's body inside a too-light gray topcoat seemed somehow smaller in the night.

"Ring the bell," Norris said. "You call out. Maybe she doesn't want to see me."

"But she was supposed to go to dinner with you?"

"That's what I thought," Norris said. "Maybe I got it wrong."

I rang the bell in the small vestibule. Nothing happened. I rang again, called out the girl's name. A door opened on an upper floor.

"Hey, stop that yellin', for Chrissake!"

The lock was a simple Yale, opened easily to one of the keys on my ring. The corridor to the rear was light and clean with new carpeting. Her apartment had a polished brass nameplate and an elegant brass knocker. Sarah Borden was doing fine. Her door had double locks and neither opened easily.

"Maybe she just put the receiver back wrong," Norris said. "It happens all the time."

Inside the apartment the light came from the room to the left at the rear, one of two rooms that overlooked the garden. The bedroom, and Sarah Borden lay on the bed. The bruises on her throat were black and purple in the small bedroom light. There was blood on the bed and on the floor. Pooled on the sheets, spattered on the walls.

Norris walked out of the bedroom.

I bent over the bed. She'd bled from at least five bullet wounds. A .38 from the look of it. Shot to pieces, and from close range, her nightgown scorched by powder burns. A pale green nightgown, bloody and ripped now, but it had been an expensive nightgown, hand-laced, daring and enticing. A special nightgown for an early evening and not to sleep in. It was twisted up under her, showing a bright green lace garter on her upper thigh. A special garter for special eyes, and the pubic hair at the center of her hips and thighs was bloody and matted. As if she had been raped too, and not a normal rape.

Out in the hall Norris was talking to himself. Talking to the walls and the sound of sleet driving against the garden windows in the silence of the apartment. Swearing at himself and the silent shadows of the hallway and the indifferent world. In the bedroom doorway I watched him for a time. He was on the floor, his back against the wall, his head down. His hands were braced flat on the floor as if to hold himself up, hold himself together, and he went on talking to the shadows and himself.

Maybe he was thinking of what he had wanted from Sarah Borden, what he had hoped to get in her apartment and in her bed. Of what he had imagined when he had looked at her the first time in Downey's. Of his own needs and plans, of what he wanted from her and what someone had taken.

I turned back into the bloody bedroom. Two armchairs and a small white table were set on a pale-blue-and-gold oriental rug in the other half of the room away from the ornate brass bed. A sitting room in the bedroom, very chic, very sophisticated, very intimate. On the table there was a silver tray with two bone china demitasse cups, a silver coffee pot, bottles of cognac and Grand Marnier, two liqueur glasses, and a plate of petit fours.

Sarah Borden had been expecting a guest in her bedroom. Dessert and coffee, her best nightgown, liqueur and brandy. A special guest. I crossed to the small table. The coffee pot was cold, the petit fours hardening and dried out where one had been cut. Probably anywhere from two to four hours ago when it had all been fresh.

I looked at the dangling phone receiver. It was on a bureau nearer the sitting-room section than the bed, but blood on the rug showed that Sarah Borden's death had not been confined to the bed. Knocked off accidentally in a struggle, or on purpose? To give a busy signal if anyone called? I wondered if maybe Norris had had an earlier date with her than he said, a different kind of date. And had kept that date.

I went out to call the police from the same bar where Norris had called me. When I returned, he still sat there in the dark hallway, alone and silent.

THIRTY

CAPTAIN PEARCE, Homicide Central, led the team that arrived. He has his own way of working. He listened to our stories without asking any questions, watched his teams for a time, then took us downtown without telling us anything. We cooled our heels an hour plus outside his office, then he summoned us in.

"You sit down, Fortune. Mr. Norris, you go with Lieutenant Castro to his office. He'll take your written statement."

Norris left with the silent Castro, who's older than Pearce and resents him. I've known Captain Pearce a year now, give or take, ever since some South American revolutionaries gunned down Captain Gazzo on a dark Eastside rooftop. Pearce inherited old Gazzo's job and his office. He's a dark blond man in a well-pressed suit, trim and compact, and the office is a lot cleaner and neater. Maybe thirty-six, he's been a captain more than two years. The new kind of cop, educated and smart, quick and efficient, without bad dreams. Almost without bad dreams. Gazzo used to say that it was always midnight in his office, and every month I can see by Pearce's eyes that it's getting later and later.

"A back window into the garden was open, the back door was locked by a Yale without a deadlock, and there was no chain on either door. No footprints or unexplained objects so far. The neighbors saw nothing, we're still questioning. Your friend Norris saw no one enter or leave not only the apartment but the building in the two hours or so he was watching from the doorway, say from eight-thirty to ten-thirty. The M.E. says she died between five and nine P.M., so that fits.''

That's the Pearce way: crisp and straight, the facts and little guesswork. Only there was something different tonight. He had taken off his suit coat and his tie, opened his shirt collar. The office was a shade less neat. Time was moving more slowly for Captain Pearce in Gazzo's old office, coming closer to that permanent midnight.

''She was shot six times. A .38, probably a six-shot revolver. He emptied the gun into her. No one heard the shots, he had to have used a silencer. She was beaten and her arm broken. He broke her arm before she died, the M.E. says, but he beat her after she died. He beat the dead body with some kind of club. We found a bloody broom handle. The M.E. says that would fit the bruises. He raped her. With the broom handle. He raped her with the broom handle after she was dead.''

Pearce lit a cigarette. He looked away from me toward the windows with their shades up and the dark city outside. I'd never seen him smoke or look out a window at nothing in particular. Some blackened stone buildings in the weak streetlights of this part of the city. A very old city down here, like Paris or London. Pearce smoked, talked to the windows.

''She had to have let him in.'' He slammed his fist against his desk, cursed the pain. I saw blood. Pearce sucked on his knuckles. ''She was all fixed up to meet him. A party. Coffee, brandy, cakes, that garter. She knew him. She knew the bastard!''

Sometimes the new cops seem colder, less human, as if they have grown up with too much horror the last half of the twentieth century, but there are some things that can still shake anyone. Captain Gazzo would have taken it as hard but differently, without the anger but with more despair. Gazzo had been alone. Pearce had a wife and two young daughters. Maybe a girl friend.

"She knew the son-of-a-bitch, Fortune." Pearce turned back toward me. "What do you know about this Steve Norris?"

I told him what I knew about Steve Norris, and about Alan and Helen Kay, but not about the kidnapping. I don't lie to the police ever, or hold back if there's any other way. This time there wasn't. I had a commitment to Ian Campbell. "She could have been in that bedroom waiting for Norris, but it doesn't feel right for a first date. It looks to me like she had the date with Norris, and then someone better came along. She wouldn't have worried about standing up a middle-aged new john. Or maybe she was set up for Norris, but someone else showed up first. Someone she liked better, or at least knew better, or maybe she planned to handle them both on the same night."

"You make her sound like a whore."

"No, just a lady who didn't like to let anyone get away from her." I told him about Jerry, the dark young man who had talked to Sarah Borden in Downey's.

Pearce took down the description and the background, flipped his intercom and instructed someone to get after Jerry, fast. Then he sat back and watched me.

"Norris could be lying all the way, Fortune. He could have gotten close to her that first night, been seeing her steadily. He could have had an earlier date than he says, killed her, left the phone hanging, and cooked up his whole story."

"He had the time," I agreed. "Calling me in to try to establish an alibi is what a killer would do."

"But you don't think he did it?"

"I can't find a motive."

"You think motive matters much in this killing?"

A killer without a motive. It scares us all, turns us cold. Because what we mean is a killer without a rational motive. All killers think they have motives. Most we can understand, can live with. But some we can't. The irrational, the unknown, the needs and hungers out of the swirling mists and dark chaos of night.

"We'll take a good look at Norris," Pearce said, looked again toward the darkness beyond his windows. "If not him, who?"

"She collected people, Captain. Never let anyone go if she could help it."

"She should have let this one go," Pearce said, and continued to watch something in the night outside his windows. "He's out there, Fortune, and he'll do it again. We've got no clues yet, no motives. All we know is that he's out there somewhere, and that he'll do it again."

"But maybe not for years," I said. "This isn't one of our mass psychos. This is someone who seems normal enough until something triggers him and he flips out, goes berserk. He might not do it again for years, maybe never."

"Unless he flips out permanently."

"That's possible," I nodded. Now I looked toward the windows and the night. "Are we so sure it's a 'he'?"

His silence was like ice. "All right, the rape could be a fake, using a broom handle. But it takes muscle to break an arm."

"Not much. She was a thin woman."

"Okay, so we don't even know that for sure. In fact, we don't know it was a psycho. That could be a fake too. But we do know she knew him or her and that's where we'll find our killer. Somewhere in her life, past or present."

I left him still staring out at his dark city of over eight million people. He knew the odds. Compared to him, I had a simple job. I just had to find out if Sarah Borden's killing had any relation to Alan Campbell and Helen Kay.

Steve Norris was waiting on a wooden bench in the main corridor. He was still pale, his hands clasped between his knees, his head down.

"It's late," I said. "You better go home."

"They think I did it, don't they?"

"Did you?"

He looked up now. "No."

"Do you have any clue to who did?"

He looked down again. "No."

"Then you better get some sleep."

He looked up once more. "Can I crash with you? It'll take me hours to get back to Chatham this late."

"Why not?"

We walked out of the echoing late-night building into the dark silence of Lower Manhattan in the small hours. Sometime since we'd found Sarah Borden dead the sleet had stopped, only the frozen slush crunching under our feet now. I walked a step behind Norris, wondered if I was going home with a killer?

THIRTY-ONE

MY REFRIGERATOR is in the kitchenette at the rear of my loft office apartment.

"There's beer, soda, and booze. I don't know what I've got to eat."

Norris sat in an armchair between the kitchen and my office up front. He laid his head back, covered his eyes with both hands. In the kitchen I opened two beers, poured them into glass mugs. I talked without looking at him.

"You hardly knew her, Norris."

"Does that mean I shouldn't feel anything? Only people we know count as people?"

"For most of us."

"God," he said.

"Take a beer," I said.

He didn't answer as I stood over him. His head turned from side to side like the slow-motion film of a man shaking his head in disbelief. Was he being excessive for a man who'd really had no more than a small hope of getting to know Sarah Borden? His hands over his eyes, he talked to the silent room.

"She should have kept her date with me. Why did she make a date with me if she had someone else around? That bedroom wasn't for me. Some other guy."

I went to my liquor cabinet and got the brandy. Presidente. Almost as good as cognac.

"Here."

He looked at the snifter. After a moment he took it. I sat behind my desk, finished my beer, and started on his. He held the brandy for some time before he drank it in a long gulp and began to talk in a different voice.

"I was a good CIA agent, a good cop. I liked being a good agent. I'm almost fifty. My wife doesn't need me, or even want me. My kids are on their own. None of them ever did really need me except for the money they had to have to live the way they had to live."

The knuckles of his large hand were white on the brandy snifter. I took it and went to refill it.

"No," he said. "I'll take the beer now."

I opened another beer. He drank from the bottle. "I didn't always like what we did in the CIA or even on the police, but I liked the work, the job, the skill. I liked the action, the importance of what I was doing, the feeling of duty, even the risk. Doing something most people couldn't. I liked the feeling I was doing something necessary." He held the bottle of beer in both his big hands. "My wife didn't like the CIA or the cops. It was too dangerous. The irregular hours were bad for the family. None of it paid enough. There wasn't much status in it, we couldn't live in the right places." He drank from the bottle of beer, wiped his mouth. "So I went to work for a big corporation in their security department. I turned out to be good at the work, good with people. I got promotions, changed companies for more money and better titles, finally joined Computer Methods, and now I'm a vice-president. I can have anything I want except the one thing I really wanted: the work I liked."

He was going over his life and feeling sorry for himself. Or trying to make up his mind to do something. Or both. I got two more beers, gave him a bottle. I poured my own into one of the glass mugs. Beer was meant to have a head. He was talking himself into doing something, or maybe trying to justify something he'd already done.

"I woke up one morning a couple of months ago and felt scared to death. I was going to die. For sure, and soon. I was going to be dead, zero. Then it hit me: I'd been zero all my life." He drank, and drank again. Shook his head. "I'd never really been anything. You know? I'd turned my back on the only thing I'd ever really wanted, the work I could feel excited about. For a nice, comfortable life with no surprises. For no life at all. I'd sold out, because that was what I was supposed to do.''

Call it the fifty horrors. Death isn't so far off anymore, and you start running. Looking for change, uncertainty, disorder. Order, certainty, leaves you with nothing to do but wait for death, the ultimate order. So you want change, action, and if you never got what you wanted you sometimes make one last grab at getting it.

''I'm burned out, Fortune. It happens all over these days. To businessmen, managers, executives.'' He drank more slowly, licked his lips. ''Most of us have an easy childhood. Protected, no real demands except to have fun. We grow up slowly, go to school without any real idea of anything we want to do except be a 'success'. It doesn't matter at what. We pick a job and work hard enough at it but it's not anything special, just another part of a normal life like a wife, kids, a house, two cars, vacations, retirement accounts. A cog in the wheel. Then you're fifty and it's not enough. They call you burned out, overworked. You're not, you're wrong worked. You're doing something you don't give a damn about, not really, because you never found anything you cared about because you never looked. Only I had something I cared about and I turned my back on it.''

If he was talking to cover up, to keep me from asking too many questions, he was doing a good job. I could hear the excitement growing in his voice, the drive, the strength. He wasn't feeling sorry for himself anymore, he was feeling eager, reliving something that had excited him.

''When I found out about Alan I thought maybe it wasn't too late after all. Maybe I could still do it. Maybe I could find Alan for Ian instead of sitting behind my damned desk every damned day. If I could bring Alan home I'd know I could still do the work. Then you showed up. I tried to outsmart you, but you caught me. Now Sarah Borden's dead, and maybe I'm not good enough anymore, but I'm out from behind that damned desk and maybe we could work together.''

It could be the truth. He had the restless tension of a man looking for something, if only a change. It fitted what he'd done so far, but, then, it would do that whether it was the truth or a fairy tale.

''We'll sleep on it,'' I said.

He leaned back in the armchair to finish his beer, his eyes closed again. He didn't act like a killer who'd just gone berserk. Then, why should he? There was a possibility that Sarah Borden's murderer wouldn't even remember having killed. But if I let him work with me, or for me, I could keep an eye on him, or at least know where he was supposed to be.

On my way to get one more beer before bed it occurred to me that maybe he wanted to keep an eye on me.

THIRTY-TWO

MY READY POT of automatic coffee was waiting for us in the morning, but we went out for breakfast to a cafeteria up near Thirty-fourth Street. I had my cold cereal and juice, and while Norris was finishing his eggs I called Kay Michaels to apologize for last night and tell her I was going to have to skip *Finnegans Wake*. I got no answer. I rang my answering service and told them to call Kay's number every half hour until they reached her and gave her the messages.

Back in my office we called Captain Pearce. He had found no witnesses, no clues, no unexplained fingerprints. The killer had been careful, or so fastidious he wore gloves on a date. They had picked up Jerry from Downey's. He had an honest alibi, so had all her other friends they'd talked to so far. Pearce wasn't happy.

"Your case is looking bigger and bigger in this, Fortune. Don't lose touch, you read me clearly?"

After I'd assured him I read him I called Ian Campbell in Chatham. The kidnappers had not contacted him. He was getting worried. He was also getting edgy, had important business to attend to, and wanted me to come out and babysit the telephone in Chatham. I had a different trip in mind. I was getting a stronger and stronger suspicion about this kidnapping.

"They should have called by now," I told him. "Listen to me, Campbell, this kidnapping is looking less and less straight. There's something more here than a simple snatch. I think our kidnappers know Alan or Helen Kay or both, knew them before the grab, and I won't find out for sure sitting out there behind a telephone. Norris is a trained man and he wants to help. I'll send him out to mother the telephone so you can do your work and I can do mine, and we can still keep in close touch."

"Knew them?"

"That's what I think."

"You want to go out to Arizona?"

"Maybe. I'm not sure what I want to do. I'll have to decide that."

"All right, send Norris out here. But, Fortune, don't make them panic. Don't lose them all again."

Norris didn't want to go, but he wasn't ready to risk his career at Computer Methods. At least, that's how he made it look. Before he left I asked him for Leah Aherne's address. That made him even more reluctant to go, but he did, and I followed right after him out of my apartment office. A thin November sun was breaking out of the high clouds by now, the slush melting into gutter rivers. The taxis were all back, I grabbed one down to Leah Aherne's address.

She lived in a loft in SoHo. That would be thanks to her father, or Ian Campbell, or both. Aspiring artists don't live in SoHo anymore. It was the top floor—the best loft—and there was no elevator. By the time I reached her door my age and condition were painfully obvious. I gave myself a couple of minutes to rebuild some image of physical stamina before ringing.

Leah Aherne opened the door herself, already turning violently away from whoever she expected me to be and didn't want to talk. "Damn you, I told you—!"

"Me you didn't tell," I said.

She looked back over her shoulder. She was wearing jeans and a black turtleneck sweater, and her hair was up and tied high with a ribbon the way a woman does when she wants to keep her hair out of something. She looked away again.

"If you're alone, *you* can come in."

"Who can't come in?"

"Anyone from Chatham!" She walked toward the distant rear of the loft. "I'm drinking, what about you?"

"Beer?"

She vanished behind a large screen. The vast loft was full of massive papier-mâché statues, columns, arches, and other stage props. There were models of stage sets on long tables, sketches pinned on the white walls, and a long row of large oil paintings in strong colors and bold shapes.

"Here."

I took my beer. She had something in a small glass more than beer. She didn't sit and she didn't tell me to sit. She walked. Around the long, echoing room. Like someone in a museum with a limited amount of time. Rapidly examining each object, model, sketch, and painting as she passed it.

"Want to talk about Chatham?" I said.

She went on walking in her long ellipse. She drank without looking at the glass. She stopped in front of the wall of her own large paintings, looked at them with cold eyes. A cold anger, not doubt, as if she hated the impulse to paint itself.

"Who kidnapped Alan and Helen Kay and why?" she said.

"I don't know who kidnapped them or why. I know they're four violent men, but I don't know who they really are or what they want."

She turned. "Money, isn't that what they want?"

"I'm not so sure."

She walked again. As if her mind could focus on Alan and Helen Kay for only a second. On anything beyond what filled her mind in the silence of her walk around and around the vast room with its bright colors and giant shapes.

I said, "You talked to Ian Campbell."

There was a stiffness to her walk. Somewhere inside her where the motion began she was rigid.

I said, "You talked to your father."

She turned the small glass of brown liquid rapidly in her long, slim hands. A manic movement of the hands around the glass.

"I knew there was something more on Ian's damned mind. And, oh boy, was there ever! All the time he was screwing me!" Her hands went around and around with the glass. "I'll bet that's why Alan ran out. He knew and didn't want any part of it! With a father like Ian he didn't want any part of Chatham or the company!

"If he knew, why not tell your father?"

She was in no mood for reason or logic. "Then he fought Ian and Ian sent him away! The son-of-a-bitch would do anything to get his way!"

"So why hire me to bring them back?"

She had no answer to that, ignored it.

"I'd think it more likely that if Alan knew, Ian would just have shut him up one way or another."

"The arrogant bastard!" She stopped walking. The drink sloshed over in her hand. "He expects me to stay with him! He actually thinks I'll go right on screwing him! Damn! Damn! Damn!" She stared down at the almost empty drink, gulped what was left. "Take me somewhere, Dan. A drink. Lunch. Over to the river. The Flotsam. Take me to the Flotsam. We'll walk all the way up to the Flotsam."

She got a heavy pile-lined storm coat and we walked down and out into the thin sun and north through the slush. Through the SoHo streets where the immigrants once worked sixteen hours a day in windowless loft factories to make good, stylish clothes for the Anglo-Saxons of New Rochelle and Shaker Heights. Rows and rows of identical buildings with carved stone facades and long loft sweat-shops for the immigrants to provide the cheap labor for the American dream.

"You know," she said, "I really liked him."

"I know."

"I really did like him. That's what hurts! Maybe I even almost loved him."

"Then it wasn't a mistake."

"Shit," she said. "Shit!"

We turned west on Houston past the St. Anthony of Padua church in the heart of Little Italy, where the festival is still held with booths of food and bad statues and the dancing of the neighborhood. A neighborhood that spawned the Mafia because it was too hard to live honestly on the dregs of the American dream.

"The four who kidnapped Alan and Helen Kay are professionals, I think," I said. "But, somehow, I think they know Alan and Helen Kay too. I think Alan and Helen Kay know them."

As we angled northwest up Bedford Street I told her about Sarah Borden. She shivered on the narrow Greenwich Village street. "That poor girl."

I waited, but she said nothing else. She watched a couple pass hand in hand. The man's eyes were intense as he looked at the face of the woman turned up to him, her mouth open and laughing. Leah was still focusing on nothing but her own thoughts. We walked on north to Fourteenth Street and across.

"Sarah Borden came from Flagstaff the same as Helen Kay, she knew Helen Kay well," I said. "She also knew Alan, and it looks like the kidnappers have taken Alan and Helen Kay to Arizona. Somehow, Arizona and maybe Flagstaff, are part of it all."

Across Fourteenth Street and into Chelsea. Where I had grown up. The streets of a boy with a missing father and a lonely mother, with two arms then but only one narrow eye to look at the streets where the choices of what a man should do are few. And even fewer men go beyond the choices offered by their small world, so the boy found petty crime until he lost an arm and had to open his second eye. In Chelsea a one-armed man has no place and no future, and I had to look closely then and see clearly with both eyes.

"Helen Kay has a brother," I said. "What do you know about him? Older or younger? Does he have a name? What does he do? Do you know what he looks like?"

We turned west toward the river, where kids still take forbidden swims on the steamy days of a New York summer. I'd gone far from these streets over the years, been up and down, but never found many more choices so came back to where I could, maybe, make some small change in the world I'd been given. And Chelsea itself had been up and down and was now up once more with renovated apartments, exorbitant rents, the young and well paid moving in.

"Her brother?" Leah said. "I don't know. He's older, I think. She never mentioned his name. Just that she had an older brother she didn't really know because they grew up handed around from different relatives to different foster homes all over Flagstaff. I don't know what he looks like."

On a street of crumbling warehouses we reached the river. Here Chelsea had not risen again yet, but it would. New York is all change. Change and loss. Every New Yorker knows that, sooner or later, everything changes, everything is lost.

"A small man, J.J., leads the kidnappers." I described J.J., Dog, the Indian, and as much as I had seen of the limousine driver. "Did you see any of them while you looked for Alan?"

Inside the Flotsam there was a waiting line for lunch. We chose the bar. She had Scotch. I had another beer. It was early, but she was in no mood to drink alone.

"I don't know, maybe that little man was outside the Hotel Emerson the night you ran into me in their room. Only he was wearing some kind of cowboy outfit. Hat, boots, a string tie."

That had the sound of J.J. Flamboyant, drawing attention to himself. Not the M.O. of a kidnapper. Maybe it was reverse psychology—a man so obvious, so eccentric, could never be a dangerous criminal. But she had a different man on her mind.

"Why did Ian do it, Dan?"

"He wants something."

"What?"

"Success," I said. "Victory. King of the hill."

"Some victory! Some damned hill! A two-bit company no one would miss if it had never been started."

"It's the only victory he's got."

"Father and daughter." She drank her Scotch. All of it.
"Dan? Come back with me. To the loft. Now and all
night."

Or was J.J. just a small city gangster, the eccentric act to
scare people with the fear of the different, the unpredictable? Or was he really eccentric, erratic, irrational?

"Do you want another Scotch?" I said.

"No. Dan? Stay with me. Today and tonight."

There was only one way to find out what J.J. was.

"I'm a lot more impressive with my clothes on than off,"
I said, smiled. "You don't want me."

"Is that no?"

"I've got a job, Leah. I have to go out of town."

"When did you decide that?"

"You don't need another old man."

"Where? Arizona?"

"Probably."

She nodded. "I'll have that Scotch now."

I had another beer I didn't need, then put her into a taxi.
I took another to my office. She was too young for me, and
she was using me to hate Ian Campbell. But I wondered if I
would have turned her down, job or no job, if Kay Michaels hadn't been there uptown?

In my apartment I checked the next flight for Phoenix,
and packed a bag. Then I called Campbell's home number.
Steve Norris answered. The kidnappers still hadn't called.

THIRTY-THREE

THERE IS NOTHING much to look out at on a jet, so I dozed
and thought about it all again. What were they waiting for?
And why go to Arizona? Most kidnappers I'd ever heard of
stayed close to the source of the ransom. A new wrinkle?

The modern snatch, no need to stay close with jets and di
rect-dialed long-distance telephones?

Or maybe it was a double squeeze. Leah Aherne had said
Helen Kay's brother was older, maybe he had money. One
ransom in New Jersey, another in Arizona? Dog took them
out to Flagstaff to bite the brother; J.J. stayed in New York
to handle Ian Campbell.

Only why were they still silent?

We landed in Phoenix at 4:00 P.M. I picked up my bag
and showed the photos of Alan and Helen Kay to the bag
gage attendants. I described J.J., Dog, and the Indian. They
didn't recall any of them on the late flight from New York
two nights ago.

No one at the ticket counters remembered them. None of
the porters could help.

One gate attendant thought maybe he might remember a
party like that around the time of the late flight from New
York. The other attendants had other concerns, were unin
terested.

A bartender in the lounge nodded. "I sure remember that
big black son-of-a-bitch. I got nothin' against 'em, you
know, long as they ain't pushy bastards. This one he order
three beers 'n' a Jack Daniel's. He pays with a hundred
chugs his Daniel's before the waitress can pick up the tray
tells me to shake my ass 'n' refill it! Smart-ass son-of-a
bitch."

"Where did they go from the lounge?"

"Who the hell cares."

"Four of them, not five?"

"Three beers 'n' a Daniel's is all I know."

The red Lincoln limousine had to be still in New York
They might have had another car, or been picked up, bu
somehow I didn't think so. I checked through the renta
counters and hit pay dirt at Hertz.

"Rented a Buick, best car we got," the Hertz man said. "They rented here before. Lots of times. Mr. King and the Indian, I mean. Usually got another guy with them, small guy, only he wasn't with 'em this time."

"The black guy's name is King?"

"Mr. D. King, right."

I showed him the photos of Alan and Helen Kay.

"They were in the party. You don't forget a lady looks like that."

"Where did they say they were going?"

"Where they always go, Flagstaff."

I said, "Rent me your cheapest automatic with a wheel shift, and everything else on the floor."

J.J. had not come from New York with them. I got an overused Chevy and drove out of Phoenix.

You rise slowly from the desert floor, from the heat of Phoenix and Rock Springs even late on a November afternoon, into the mountains and the pine forests. Straight north on I-17 to Camp Verde and the forests and on up into the mountains to Flagstaff and the snow.

It's a beautiful drive. Heat and desert and dust and forest and mountain and snow all in one afternoon. A wild land that is always beautiful because it is wild. The desert with its distances and jagged isolation, the remote emptiness of heat where a hawk soars alone and a lizard runs and the bridges cross only stones. The towering pines and the long sweep of mountain valleys buried in snow to the vast sky, where the wolf once hunted and the cougar still does far off at the dark edge of the pines. Only people destroy beauty.

It was dark when I turned off the highway into the streets of Flagstaff, packed with snow and ringed by the mountain-pine slopes. The Hertz office was still open.

"Yeh," the agent said, "Dog King turned the Buick in yesterday morning." His feet were up on his desk, a stove hot in the corner. "Broke a damned spring out in that damned old mining camp of theirs. Guess I'm lucky it wasn't an axle. Takes a tank to get in and out of that canyon.''

''Were the others with him?''

''That Indian, never heard his name, and a young feller I don't know. Everyone here knows Helen Kay Murdoch. Ain't seen her in a couple or three years. Never figured she got along with Jasper that good.''

''Jasper?''

''Jasper Murdoch, her big brother. Not that he ain't as small as she is. He owns old High Point Camp out in Little Chee Canyon, where Dog King and that Indian works for him.''

''What does Jasper Murdoch look like?''

He described the small man, J.J., to the last quirk.

''Who's got jurisdiction out at this High Point Camp?''

''Sheriff, I guess.''

THIRTY-FOUR

THE YOUNG DEPUTY on duty listened to my story, took my credentials, and told me to wait. After he used the telephone, he spent a lot of time looking at my low suede boots. At least it wasn't my arm.

He was amused. ''You sure ain't gettin' far out to High Point Camp in them shoes this time o' year. No way.''

The older man who soon came in had to be the sheriff himself, from his worn western boots to his white Stetson. He took my credentials from the deputy, turned them over in his big hands as if that would shed light on my story.

''Sheriff Gwynne,'' he said finally. ''You're Fortune?''

''Dan Fortune. From New York,'' I said. ''Do they call this Jasper Murdoch J.J. too?''

"Sometimes. What do you want with Murdoch?"

"I want to get his sister back from him. And her husband."

"Yeh," the sheriff nodded, "we heard Helen Kay got married. Back East somewhere. She's been gone away for maybe three years."

"She's back," I said. "With her husband."

"Yeh, I did hear something like that," Sheriff Gwynne agreed. "Why would you be wanting Helen Kay?"

"Because I was hired to bring them back to New Jersey. Actually, it's Alan Campbell I was hired to bring back, that's Helen Kay's husband. His father hired me."

"We ain't got much interest in the husband."

"But you do in the Murdochs," I said. "Enough to get you up off the couch at home, right? What's so interesting to the police about the Murdochs?"

He got up and motioned for me to follow him. We went down a long corridor off the main room and up to the second floor. He closed the door of his private office behind him, motioned me to a chair, took a seat in his own high-backed desk chair behind his desk. He didn't swivel; he rocked.

"We ain't especially interested in Helen Kay, except to see how she's gonna turn out. Now Jasper.... He do anything back in New York?"

"To tell you the truth," I lied, "I'm not sure." And I told him most of the story up until just before the kidnapping. He just stared at me. I wasn't impressing him.

"You just want to take this Alan Campbell home to his daddy?"

"That's about the size of it. The problem is he doesn't seem to want to come home, and you haven't told me what's so interesting to the police about the Murdochs."

He rocked in the desk chair. Sometimes I think we're a nation of nervous habits, neurotic tics. Maybe a world. The sheriff wasn't buying my story all the way. All policemen develop a sense of knowing when something isn't true. His problem was to smoke me out without telling me anything he didn't want to.

"Maybe nothing," he said. "How much do you know about Jasper Murdoch? Or J.J. if you want."

"Just that he's Helen Kay's older brother. I don't even know what he does for a living."

He rocked some more. "A lot of Murdochs around this part of the state. Most of 'em are solid enough if kind of restless. Old Jock Murdoch, the grandfather, was a back-canyon prospector who never did settle down or own anything he couldn't pack on his back. Had seven boys, all brought up by three different mothers. Like any passin' tomcat, wouldn't bet he ever said 'hello' to the mothers. No one ever did know when old Jock died or where. Probably back in some mountain cave like any animal."

He paused for effect, looking for any contribution to the conversation I might give. I gave him a smile. He shrugged.

"Well, all seven of those boys grew up wild, ran around over three counties. But most of 'em got married in the end, settled down, worked at more-or-less steady jobs. All except Sam Murdoch. He came out bad. In and out of prison all his life. Stole horses, rustled cattle in Mexico, smuggled wetbacks down to the border, ran dope across too. He was only twenty-eight when he got killed in a shoot-out in Agua Prieta. He'd married a dropout from North Arizona U. They had Jasper early, Sam was never around, the girl drifted into working in bars. Had Helen Kay not long before Sam died, and pretty soon the mother took off and never came back."

I began to understand Helen Kay Campbell. Her reckless partying, her hustling. The street urchin with the model's face and body.

"The two kids were passed around from uncles to cousins, mostly split up from each other 'cause Jasper was nine, ten years older. After a while they ran out of relatives who'd take 'em, I guess, got sent on through foster homes. Helen Kay was always runnin' off and gettin' dragged back, Jasper was in and out of hospitals after he got mauled by a bear out huntin' with one of his uncles. I guess you'd say they had to turn out bad, look at things kind of different."

"You know a lot about them," I said.

He nodded slowly. "Okay, Fortune. The trouble is they didn't get better when they grew up. Helen Kay and her boyfriends raising all kinds of hell till we was glad to see the back of her when she left town. A lot of bad stuff going down around this county and the next counties we think leads right out to High Point Camp and Jasper and his friends."

"What kind of bad stuff?"

"Well, start with how Jasper got High Point Camp. It belonged to his last foster family. Seven years ago both the man and his wife died in an accident that was awful funny, only we couldn't prove anything, and Jasper turned out to inherit the camp. Since then we've had hijackings, burglaries out in Sedona, some extortion, and a lot of car theft. We know they're behind most of it, we haul them in all the time. So far we haven't made anything stick. Jasper Murdoch's smart, they operate outside Flagstaff, only come back to High Point Camp to hole up."

"They would be J.J., Dog, that Indian, and someone who drives the red limo?"

Gwynne nodded.

"Tell me about Dog King. How'd he get that nickname?"

"It ain't a nickname," Gwynne said. "His dad trained the best hound dogs and bird dogs in the state, never had a first name anyone knew so we just called him Hound Dog. I

guess he had a sense of humor 'cause he named the boy
Hound Dog King, Jr.! That black boy grew up worse'n even
Sam Murdoch, served a prison term before he was fourteen. Took up boxing in prison, went pro out in California,
then did time in San Quentin or Soledad, never knew which.
Worked his damn way back to us through L.A. and Ve-
gas—bodyguard, strong-arm man, hijacker, contract killer.''

"Nice guy," I said. "How about the Indian?"

"Never have heard any name on that Indian, not even a
tribe. Looks kind of like a Tuba City Navajo, but doesn't act
like the People. Could be southern Ute, or any damned tribe
as far as I can tell. Damned if I know the difference.''

"And the fourth guy? The driver of the limousine?"

"Flaco Sanchez and about fifty aliases. Con man, gam-
bler, fence, smuggler. You name it, Flaco's done it somewhere along the border. Spent half his life in prison
somewhere."

"You make them sound like a minor crime wave."

"They are," Gwynne said, rocked some more in his chair.
"You sure your business out here doesn't have something to
do with some action they pulled back east?"

"Not that I know," I evaded.

"You're not after Murdoch and his pals?"

"Not yet, Sheriff." It left me an out for later when I might
need his help.

"You just want this Alan Campbell? Helen Kay's husband?"

"As far as I know."

His eyes told me he heard my evasions, but he didn't push
it just now.

"What do you want from me?"

"Well, Alan doesn't want to come back east. Maybe if I
knew more about Helen Kay and J.J. it would help me convince him."

The sheriff considered that for a time, looking at it from all sides to see if I had any angle that could harm him.

"Okay. You want to know about Helen Kay go to Ginger Karas," he gave me the address. "Jasper's harder. He's been on his own a lot longer, and, like I said, his last foster family's dead. I ain't sure who had him before that. Ginger Karas can tell you some about Jasper, but probably not a hell of a lot."

I got her telephone number too, thanked him, and got up. He stopped me.

"If you maybe do decide you want to go after Jasper and his pals, Fortune, you tell me, right? High Point Camp's no place to go alone."

I nodded, and went out to my rented car. I drove to the Ramada Inn, checked in, and called Ginger Karas. There was no answer. By New York time it was late, but I called Ian Campbell in Chatham anyway. A woman's voice answered. One of his secretaries. No one had called about Alan or money, she didn't know where Mr. Campbell or Mr. Norris were, and Mr. Aherne had left the company. Ian Campbell didn't waste time.

I called Kay Michaels. No answer. She was a big girl enjoying a visit to New York; it didn't bother me. Or only a little. I went on calling Ginger Karas for two hours while I watched a basketball game between the University of New Mexico and Brigham Young. It made me feel a long way from New York. The Karas number never answered. I went to bed. I felt lonely. Motel beds are too big alone, too smooth, too new.

THIRTY-FIVE

IN THE MORNING I had a good breakfast in a local diner, hungry from the mountain air. I sat at a window and looked out at the cold, brilliant winter sun that reflected a dazzling glare from the deep snow on the ground all through the mountain town. After coffee I called Ginger Karas again. She was home, told me to come right on over, sounded as bright as the glare of the sun from the snow. The mountain air again.

As I followed the directions to Ginger Karas's house, I saw most of the private houses were on hills north of the railroad tracks, haphazard on the snow-deep slopes, rural with roads up from the main highway, the business streets, and the railroad. Unremarkable houses, not shabby exactly but routine, dull and comfortable, unkempt and unpretentious. South of the tracks was Northern Arizona University, and north I could see the mountains, the high San Francisco peaks.

Ginger Karas lived on a barren slope at the northern edge of town in an unpainted gray frame house that looked like a cardboard model cut out and stuck on the land. There were some outbuildings, and the yard was littered with twisted shapes covered now by the snow. Where the snow had blown clear, the dark earth looked like a scar.

The woman who answered my ring was as cardboard as the house. Part of nothing, not even herself. Bits and pieces of what everyone she had ever met told her she was. In her early sixties, I judged, too skinny, bleached blond hair, heavy lipstick of a bright red shade, three-inch spike heels with sling backs that flopped on her feet, her hair actually in curlers, and wearing a flowered housedress. Heavy over it all a thick beige cardigan with a high roll collar because it was cold. A smiling woman.

"That's me, sure enough. Ginger Karas. Muriel I was named, but no one's called me nothin' but Ginger in forty years."

I asked about Helen Kay and Jasper Murdoch.

"Never knew Jasper much, heard about him some, but Helen Kay I raised like my own. Not that she gives me anything for that, not her."

"She didn't like living with you?"

"Can't say she liked or didn't."

She tottered a little on the spike heels, and her eyes were worn. I had a hunch she'd had a big night in some local bar last night. From the curlers in her hair she meant to have another tonight. Probably a regular in some local tavern, one of the boys. It was a long, cold winter in Flagstaff. She dropped heavily into a faded red velvet armchair, waved me to the couch. I sat. She smiled at me.

"Can't say Helen Kay liked it any worse here than any other place she lived, or any better neither. She's just plain a mean girl, Helen Kay, a chip on her shoulder and cold. Except, o' course, with the boys and her motorbikes."

"How long did you have her, Mrs. Karas?"

"Call me Ginger, I like it better, you know?" She blinked as if she'd lost something. "Oh, yeh, let's see, how long'd I have her? Not all that long. Maybe from about thirteen till sixteen, yeah. Right up until she ran off."

"She left Flagstaff at sixteen?"

"She left me. She left town too, mostly, but she come back sometimes, you never knew, you know? Right after school let out the summer she was sixteen. Not that she went to school much, but her best boyfriend was graduatin' that year."

"She was popular with the boys?"

"Wanted to be."

"Did she leave anything behind I could look at?"

"Sure did."

"Can I see her room?"

Ginger Karas nodded, heaved herself up from the sagging red velvet, and led me through the house to some rear stairs. It was an old house, in need of paint, wallpaper, and repair, but she was a meticulous housekeeper. Somehow, that didn't fit what she looked like. You never knew about people. Helen Kay's room on the second floor was as cold and neat as a monk's cell.

"Can't stand mess, you know, always made her keep her junk out in the old shed. God, that girl could collect crap."

"Is it still in the shed?" I asked. "Her junk?"

"Far as I know, never go out there myself. If you mean to go look, you better wear Karas's old boots."

Down in the barren but immaculate kitchen the high black rubber boots were two sizes too big for me. The kitchen was obviously used now to cook for only one, yet Ginger Karas didn't seem especially sad or lonely. Indifferent, if anything. Maybe Helen Kay hadn't had much reason to be grateful for living here.

"Karas always did have big feet," she said, laughed.

I crossed the deep snow of the yard through muddy spots where the sun had melted the snow in patches blown thin by the wind. In the shed there were some tools hanging on one wall. On the other three walls were hundreds of magazine covers, illustrations clipped from magazines, photographs of young and not-so-young men cut from the same magazines. Motorcycle and racing-car magazines, open-road magazines. Some old glossies of famous drivers, all signed with a flourish. Illustrated maps. Photos of bearded Hell's Angels and other gaudy motorcycle gangs. Endless landscapes of distances, of open roads that led toward infinite horizons, of mountains and purple deserts.

I looked at the walls of clippings and photos for some time. The shed was like a church full of icons. Dream and refuge. Wheels, the open road and freedom. The men and the machines and the path. The good life for Helen Kay, or even life itself, and I remembered the oil on the bedroom floor of the house in Chatham. I looked for any sign of a motorcycle itself. There was a dusty workbench strewn with various neglected parts of motorcycles, but no actual motorcycle. Only a battered motocross bicycle.

I went outside again and walked around the entire shed. There was no evidence of any motorcycle. But in the open space between the shed and a tumbledown chicken coop even under the snow I could see the shapes of banked turns and jumps of what looked like a home-made dirt bike or motocross practice course. Probably motocross bicycling, it all looked too small and flimsy for a motorcycle layout.

I trudged back through the snow—dazzling under the bright winter mountain sun—took the boots off on the back porch. Inside, Ginger Karas had made a pot of coffee. In front of the almost empty refrigerator she stood holding a can of beer as if trying to make a decision. There was a lot of beer in the refrigerator. She questioned me with the heavy liner of her eyebrows.

"Coffee for me," I said.

She hesitated. "Ah, to hell with it."

She grinned and popped the can of beer. She sipped at it while she poured my coffee. I took cream and sugar, I've stopped trying to impress people with my sophisticated taste. Ginger Karas turned her coffee cup upside down in the saucer, sat down across the kitchen table with her beer. Her coffee was good.

"Did Helen Kay ever have a motorcycle?"

"Sure, lots. She went after every boy had one. She never had any trouble getting the boys, or getting the boys to do about what she wanted."

"But not one of her own?"

"Her own boy?"

"Her own motorcycle."

She drank her beer. "Nope. She never could save the money, and poor old Karas wasn't about to buy her one."

"But she wanted one?"

"So bad she could taste it. Motorcycles and boys, that's all she ever thought about as far as I could ever tell." She drank and sighed happily. A woman who enjoyed her beer. "Between you and me I think the bike was more important to her than the boys. She ran off more 'n' once with some bum kid on a motorcycle, but she always came back."

"You said she came back a few times after she first ran off. Was she on a motorcycle those times? With a boy?"

"Nope, always came back on the bus and alone. She usually left on a bike with a boy, though. New boy, new bike."

Ginger Karas had finished her can of beer, abandoned all pretense. She got up, took another can from the rows in the refrigerator, looked at me. I shook my head, poured myself a fresh cup of coffee. I had the feeling the two beers weren't her first of the day. If she were a regular in some tavern at night, it could add up to a lot of beer.

"What about Jasper Murdoch?" I asked.

She stood at the refrigerator drinking the beer. "He's nine, maybe ten years older, we never saw him much. When he did come around he never talked. If you'd talk to him he just looked at you. Moved around like a shadow, you never heard him until he just sort of appeared, you know? I mean, he was creepy. Some people was always sure he was a retard." She was drinking the beer now like a real beer drinker with a thirst, opened another can. "Something awful funny the way that last foster family o' his got theirselves killed in that accident."

"He had an accident himself, right? In the hospital a lot when he was a boy?"

She nodded. "Yeh, I heard that. When he was around twelve, I think, before we got Helen Kay, so I don't know much about it. Got chewed on by a cougar or maybe a bear out huntin' with one o' the Murdochs. Guess they had to sew him up all over, but I never saw no scars, so I guess he got healed up okay."

She was drinking the beer now as if nothing in the whole world had ever tasted so good and she was afraid the world would run out of it before she got her share. Her eyes were going slack and lidded as she sat down again with her fourth can of beer and smiled vaguely at me across the kitchen table.

"There can be scars you don't see," I said.

She drank. "That's horseshit. I heard that stuff 'n' it's all crap. Egghead stuff. A scar's a scar. You see it, you know it."

I was losing her. "Was Jasper ever in any kind of mental hospital? Asylum?"

She shook her head, drank again. "He ain't crazy, just a creepy little punk. Around here people're scared of him. They got scared when his foster folks got killed, 'n' a couple of kids he used to hang out with, 'n' they say he's a real gangster now, but he don't scare me, nosir."

She was becoming incoherent all at once the way alcoholics do, from seeming sobriety to collapse between one drink and the next. I stood up.

"Thanks for the coffee and the help."

She waved her arm, her eyes looking somewhere to my left, *"De nada."*

As I left the kitchen she laid her head down on the table, curlers, makeup, and all. She would probably sleep the rest of the day, that was how she managed the tavern nights. Winter was long and small in Flagstaff, not a lot of choices.

If Helen Kay's other foster families or Murdoch relatives were anything like Ginger Karas, maybe she'd had a reason for dreaming of motorcycles and the open road.

It was pushing lunchtime as I drove back to the Ramada Inn, but I wasn't hungry and it was time I called Chatham. Ian Campbell himself answered at once.

"They called."

"When?"

"Noon on the nose. That one called J.J. And, Fortune, there was something familiar about his voice. I've heard that voice somewhere before."

Ten A.M. Arizona time. Two hours ago. If J.J., or Jasper Murdoch, had called from Arizona. I didn't tell Campbell what had been familiar about Jasper's voice. Not yet.

"What did he say?"

"I get two hundred and fifty thousand and bring it out to Phoenix. I rent a car and check in at the Desert Wind Motel in Camp Verde, wherever that is."

"A small town on the road to Flagstaff. Go on."

"I wait at the motel for their contact. There won't be a drop of the money, and later I get Alan back. It'll be an exchange. I bring the cash, they bring Alan and his wife, and we meet out in the open, where they'll know right away if there are any cops or tricks. If they spot anything out of line, they'll kill Alan and Helen Kay and vanish into the hills. He told me not to think they couldn't vanish because this would be their backyard and they could."

"They could," I agreed. "When will you fly out?"

"Tonight," Campbell said. "Fortune? I told them I had to see Alan and Helen Kay before I brought any cash."

It was how I had expected him to act from the start, son or no son. Tough and hard-nosed. But he hadn't. Too quick to give in to the kidnappers, too tough now. A contradiction, and I don't like contradictions. What had happened, changed? Or what was I missing?

"That was damned risky for Alan."

His voice missed a beat. "I have to see him."

"What did J.J. say?"

"He didn't want to, but I held my ground and he finally greed. But he said he'd arrange it. When I'm at the Desert Vind Motel someone will pick me up. I'll be taken to meet Jan, then brought back. After that I'm to have the money the room, and they'll contact me again for the exhange."

Jasper Murdoch and his men had to feel pretty secure and onfident out at High Point Camp. Maybe in the whole ate. The smaller an area, the better a crook or a business-an can control it.

"They didn't say anything about what I should do?"

"They didn't mention you at all."

That was funny too. I was the only one they'd contacted p to now, I was sure to be close to Campbell, why not have e take some part, use me? Did they know where I was? Campbell's voice from the other end of the line broke me ut of my reverie.

"Fortune? I asked if you'd found them out there?"

"Yeh, I found them."

"In Flagstaff?"

"Yes," I said. "Campbell, listen. I told you there was omething wrong about this kidnapping. That J.J. you alked to is Jasper Murdoch, Helen Kay's brother."

There was a breathing silence at the other end of the line.

"That's why his voice was familiar to you," I said. "You alked to him after they disappeared from Chatham. You ld him they'd run off, told him you wanted them to come ome. I think that's what gave Murdoch the idea of hold-ig them for ransom."

"Brother?" Ian Campbell's voice said.

"You gave them the whole idea. I'll bet on it."

"I warned Alan about that Helen Kay! She's part of it!"

"Maybe she is," I said. "Maybe Alan is too. Both work
ing with Jasper to con money out of you. Or maybe the
don't even know they've been kidnapped. Maybe Murdoc
just told them some story, offered them something, to ge
them to come out here with him and they don't even know
he's asking for ransom."

"Does that mean you think they're really not in any dan
ger at all?"

It didn't mean that at all. Even if they were involved in th
scheme, I didn't think they were safe around Jasper Mur
doch, Dog, and the Indian. And if they weren't part of it
were being fooled, I didn't want to think about their safet
when they found out what was really going on.

"I wouldn't bet on it, Campbell," I said.

"Her own brother?"

"Her own brother," I said.

I didn't add that if they had agreed to let him see Alan, i
had to mean that Alan and Helen Kay knew they were being
ransomed. The only question left was: were they part of th
extortion on Campbell, or, sister or no sister, was it a rea
kidnapping?

"Steve Norris wants to come with me," Campbell said.

"Why?"

"He says to help. I'll need someone to hold the money
while I go to meet Alan."

Norris wanted action. I wondered if it was his only rea
son for wanting to be with Ian Campbell.

"Okay," I said. "I'll try to meet you at the Desert Wind
tonight. But if I don't, you and Norris follow Murdoch'
instructions. And, Campbell, follow them to the letter."

THIRTY-SIX

THE ONLY FOUR-WHEEL drive vehicle with an automatic transmission they had at Hertz was a new Jeep without a top. They really didn't want to rent it to me. The manager looked at my feet.

"I'll get some snow boots," I said.

"You better get some extra sweaters too, a sleeping bag, a tent, food, and snowshoes if you figure on leaving the Jeep."

If he was that nervous, I decided it wouldn't be a good idea to tell him it was High Point Camp and Little Chee Canyon I was planning to drive out to.

"You got a rifle?" he asked.

"Do I need one?"

"If you do you won't have time to come back and get one," he said. "Rent one down to the hardware store. I'll put a can of drinking water in the Jeep."

They had boots as well as rental rifles at the hardware store. I drew the line at the sleeping bag and snowshoes, but stopped at a grocery for some meat, bread, and chocolate bars, then got on the road before they scared me out of going. Little Chee Canyon was north, and the blacktop county road wasn't all that good from the start. But when I turned off into the canyon itself I began to understand why the Hertz man had been worried.

The road into the silent canyon was little more than a dirt track under the deep snow. Two narrow ruts in the snow showed that some people did drive out here, but not many.

I drove slowly, following the ruts deeper into the canyon under the steep sides of rock and snow. Twisting upward among the thick pines, the road wound above a dark, rush-

ing creek of black water spewing white over rocks. The high
slopes seemed to close in until it was as dark as twilight
From time to time the road crossed the surging creek or
narrow bridges of wood and logs that gave off a hollow,
echoing sound from the canyon walls. I drove slower and
slower as the tortuous road continued upward through the
silence of the tall trees and the roar of the creek.

After rising steadily for over half an hour, the road suddenly leveled, the creek widened, and the canyon opened
into a small basin of flat land with the higher peaks behind
it. A high mountain valley dazzlingly bright with the winter
afternoon sun on the snow. On the distant slopes across the
creek I saw the ruins of old frame buildings: mine en-
trances, storage sheds, old sluices on feeders that flowed
down to the creek. Decayed stone huts and log shacks scat-
tered across the far slopes.

It had to be High Point Camp, and from the cover of a
grove of blue spruce I searched the slopes. All I could see
were the ruins with no signs of life. Ahead, the road and the
creek disappeared around a low bluff that came down almost to the edge of the creek. I drove the Jeep into the
spruce grove and walked ahead through the trees. In the
shadows of the trees I felt the cold down to the bone. The
Hertz man knew what he was warning about. At night, the
cold would move in as deadly as a giant steel scythe.

When I reached the bluff I saw that the road curved
sharply around it. I had no way of knowing what was
around the curve. Slipping, puffing, hanging onto trees and
bushes with my lone arm, I hauled and crawled my way up
the bluff through the snow. Behind the bushes on the crest,
I peered out at the high valley. Directly in front of me the
road and creek swung in a big curve through the widest part,
and a cluster of buildings stood on either side of the creek
with a narrow, swaying footbridge across the creek between them.

There was a frame church with a skeleton steeple and no roof, a ruined hotel, some shops all collapsed at the rear, and what might have been a general store. Up the slope on the west bank was a saloon, and beyond the saloon just before the road went into the mountains on the far side a low, windowless building with half a roof and rows of collapsed bunks inside. Still farther up the slope near the saloon, almost against the mountain, a large, imposing building in good repair shined in the sun.

Three stories high, its unpainted boards glowed in the sun that reflected from the glass in all its windows. Wooden stairs came up from the saloon below to a double front door, and the front windows of the first floor had stained glass in the upper halves. There was a jaunty weather vane of a naked woman on the peak of a false-front tower, and what looked like a bathhouse wing on the bank of a feeder creek with great stone fireplaces outside for heating cauldrons of water. In its day it had dominated the rough settlement. Now smoke came from its chimney.

I worked my way through the trees and snow along the top of the bluff toward the three-story building. Until I reached an open area not far along the bluff. It had been cleared all the way down to the valley floor. On the cleared slope, wooden boards, flat rocks, and crude crosses leaned and lay fallen in ragged rows. A cemetery, Boot Hill. Weathered and worn epitaphs were carved into the grave markers: *When they jumped his claim, old Jake got em. They done the same, so long Jake—1832–1896...3 jumpers. Good riddance—?-1896...Billy Caxton, killed by a woman. Was only sixteen, didn't know no better—1882–1898...Six travelers, froze on Back Pass—1892...Ellie McCabe—1876–1904—Died of the fever and McCabe.*

The voice came from directly in front of me.

"What you want we should write for you?"

I saw the rubber boots, the pale pink pants tucked into the boots, the bottom of a thick fur coat, and raised my eyes to look at the muzzle of the Smith & Wesson .357 magnum, the thin smile and the black face of Dog.

"J.J., he's right again," Dog said. "He said this mother was a good damn sleuth."

My old pistol was in my bag at the Ramada Inn. The rented rifle was in the Jeep. And I was lucky that's where they were.

The Indian's voice was behind me. "What we do with him?"

"What we do with you, Fortune?" Dog said.

I said, "Throw me off the place for trespassing? Send me out the way I came in?"

That broke them both up. The Indian's laughter was soundless, a shaking of his squat torso in its greasy sheepskin jacket. It didn't help me. Still laughing, Dog motioned with the big .357 and I walked behind him toward the three-story building on the slope with its windows shining in the winter sun of the high valley.

The Indian followed with a .45 automatic.

THIRTY-SEVEN

INSIDE THE BUILDING a single enormous room took up most of the ground floor. Red and green sunlight through the stained-glass upper windows colored a dozen sitting areas of couches and love seats and stuffed chairs around small tables, everything in red velvet and dark wood and polished brass. There was a great deal of brass.

An ornate staircase went up to the second and third floors and divided the large sitting room from a smaller entrance room with a counter like a hotel registration desk and a long wooden bench where bellboys could have waited to take guests upstairs. But the row of polished brass key hooks, each hook with a brass room number, was at the front of the counter instead of the back, the bench was not for waiting bellboys, and the old building had not been a hotel.

J.J. Murdoch sat alone in the big room, his narrow head red and blue and green in the sunlight through the stained glass. He wore a white linen suit this time as if in the tropics, a blue striped shirt, and a planter's broad-brimmed white hat. The big custom-made tape deck was on the floor. The music was Mahler again, the Ninth Symphony. Murdoch looked at us for some time. At Dog, at the Indian, and the longest at me.

"Fortune, right? The New York private eye." He turned his inward eyes toward Dog. "How come this one's alive, Dog? You didn't snuff him?"

"You never told me to," Dog said.

Murdoch punched a button on the stereo. It became silent.

"You know, you're right. How about that?"

Dog shrugged. "You want me to do it now?"

Now I knew why Murdoch had not mentioned me to Ian Campbell. He'd thought Dog had gotten rid of me permanently. Twice now I'd lived to go on with the case by sheer chance. Then, we all stay alive day to day by a thousand chances. It's just a little more uncertain in my line of work.

"What's he doing here?" Murdoch said.

"Sneakin' around," Dog said. "We spotted him down at the highway turnoff, watched him all the way up. He stashed the car in the trees, we picked him up on Boot Hill comin' this way."

So they had a vantage point from where they could observe the highway and the road, see danger approaching. It was something to remember for next time. If there would be a next time. And I didn't really think there wouldn't be a next time. I couldn't think there wouldn't be a next time. No one can believe in his own death, not really.

Murdoch stared at me. "What the hell for, Fortune? You gonna rescue them, save Campbell's money? The money more important than his kid's life or yours?"

"It's my job to try, Murdoch."

"You got a dangerous job." He closed his eyes as if he was very tired. "So you know who we are."

"It's not hard to learn that around here."

His eyes were still closed. "Greed. To save Campbell's money you stick your neck out. Greed makes the world go round. Greed makes us free. Greed helps us all." He opened his eyes. "Dog, go check on our other visitors. Charley, watch the road."

As his gunmen left the big, sunny room, Murdoch took a snub Colt Agent revolver from the pocket of his white suit, held it in his lap. A small show of force, but I felt better with Dog out of the room anyway. Not a lot better. Murdoch spoke to the archway between the big room and the entrance where Dog and the Indian had vanished.

"Savages. Add nothing, move nothing, change nothing. All of us. No more than the goddamned apes." He weighed the gun in his small hand as if weighing us all. "We're all happy as clams to live easy on the sweat and blood of other guys. Ready and willing to be nice and safe and comfortable while most people on this fucking planet starve and die like flies."

He punched a button on his portable. Viciously. The Mahler Ninth started again. Mahler was his music. He listened, an odd, almost haunted expression in his flat eyes now. He looked toward my missing arm again, as if the empty sleeve fascinated him.

"You were a kid. How does a kid handle it, you know?"

"It happened."

"That missin' arm's made you do everything you done since."

"Something happens to everybody," I said. Then I sat down facing him. "How do we know Alan and Helen Kay aren't part of this squeeze? How do we know they're not getting a cut?"

"You don't." He heard me, answered me, but he wasn't thinking about me. "Your whole fucking life, that arm."

"If they're part of it, why should Campbell pay?"

"'Cause he don't know for sure. Nobody don't ever know nothing for sure." He brooded, somehow isolated in the music and warm sunlight of the old bordello waiting room. "You married, Fortune? You got kids?"

"No," I said. "On both."

"Why?"

"Who ever knows, Murdoch? The ones I wanted said no, the ones said yes I didn't want."

"Bullshit. You got two arms you got a home, a family. You ain't got, you don't get. If you ain't just like all of them you're nothing. You got nothing you get nothing."

"That's an easy excuse," I said. "Real easy."

You could never be sure when he heard you or when he didn't, when he was talking to you and when he wasn't. When he was talking to someone else, maybe someone who wasn't even there, or maybe to himself. In that private world where only he lived, hearing some unseen voice. Somehow different this time, restless, even agitated. Hearing the voice of Mahler. "All neat, that was the nineteenth century. A place for everyone. Rules and order. The twentieth is chaos. Mahler's chaos. All dark and crazy, a couple of billion dead bodies up ahead!" He stared at the chaos ahead.

I said, "The arm never stopped me doing what I wanted to do."

"Because you stopped yourself. You stopped wanting what you couldn't get. What if you never stopped wanting?

What if they laugh at you, call you a freak, push you out, and even then you don't stop wanting?''

He hit a button on the stereo and the music cut off. Its echo hung in the dusty room as Jasper Murdoch sat rigid, listened to that voice only he could hear. Or to a different sound.

"What did you want you couldn't get?" I said.

He raised the stubby Colt and fired three shots. One at a time. Carefully. Squeezed them off, and smashed three lamps one after the other across the wide room.

Dog stood in the archway. He had his pistol. He looked toward the smashed lamps, and then at Murdoch.

"Nice shootin'."

Murdoch nodded at me, "Take him out of here."

"How far?"

"Second floor. He can talk to Campbell."

I walked ahead of Dog out through the archway and up the stairs to the second floor. Behind me I heard three more shots. Something more smashed. The music began again. Mahler. The end of his last symphony, fading softly away into silence.

THIRTY-EIGHT

THE ROOM WAS small and dark. Mahler faded away again and again far below. There was no way out of the room. I sat on the narrow bed against the wall and hoped I would never hear the end of Mahler again. I held my hand tight over one ear and tried not to listen with the other. Even silence is hard for a one-armed man.

I knew there was no way out because the first thing I had done after Dog locked the door was search the small room. There was an empty closet that smelled of dry grass and field rats and empty snail shells that crunched under my feet. There were no lights. A narrow iron bed, two musty armchairs in the vague light from the snow below. Two narrow windows and heavy oak shutters brought to the frontier valley long ago at great expense to awe the clients in their filthy, rancid sheepskins and awkward spurs. The shutters, nailed now, only a feeble light through the slats from the snow below.

The single door locked solid. A heavy oak door, carved ornate and shipped with the shutters from somewhere East to the cheers of the randy miners. Not just the flesh for the dog-dirty in from the creeks, but elegance and style, a touch of civilization. With the hinges outside.

Nothing in the dark room to break down a door, pull heavy nails from shutters.

No holes in floor or ceiling.

Walls.

After a time you give up.

On the narrow iron bed I waited for the faint, distant Mahler to end again. Hand over my ear, trying to hide from the sound. Waiting for what would come, be done to me. For Mahler to end again, and finally, to be over.

Then?

Did I want Mahler to end? Murdoch to remember me, to think about me? To turn to Dog, give his orders?

A killer. The way another man is an engineer, a drinker, left-handed. Dog. And proud of the name. Mad Dog. Wild Dog. Devil Dog King. King Dog. A killer for hire. For the gold medallions and the silk shirts, the good, rich life. A killer to live, for hire and for fun. The happy man is the man who enjoys his work. Or only indifferent. The professional. A matter of skill and judgment. Cool in hand and eye. Cold. Efficient. And, finally, not really sane.

No more sane than Jasper Murdoch, J.J. Brother and boss, kidnapper and extortionist, music lover and lecturerto-the-universe and hearer of unseen voices. Half educated and half crazy. Who had stared at my missing arm from the first moment at the stone bridge over the Passaic in front of Ian Campbell's house and talked of things that were lost. Of new worlds and chaos. What had he lost? His parents? His childhood? His place in a cold world that didn't want him? His chance in an indifferent world? A man outside who lived to wreak revenge on "them"? A guilty universe? More than half insane and the leader of a killer, and an Indian who sucked beer and belonged nowhere, and a skinny old outlaw of the border.

And who would come for me?

In a dark room waiting for the action of others.

And sooner or later time slips away, loses its meaning in the dark room where you can only wait. The light fades through narrow slits, grows darker, and there is no more time. When the light finally returns which return is it? The first? The fourth? The thousandth? Only a darkening and a lightening, and all the distant noises are today or maybe yesterday. Is the softly ending Mahler the Mahler of today or ten days ago or ten months from now? Are the voices, somewhere far off, new voices or old voices, and do you know the faces? Are there really voices?

In the power of others.

They sit or stand. All around you. Watch you smiling or cold-faced blank with hate, their hands slowly opening and closing.

Helpless, you wait.

For whatever they will do. To you.

In their hands. Hanging in heavy, thick hands. From piano wire. Bullet in the back of the head. A short knife in the dark. Cease to exist. Never found. Gone and nothing is ever known. Without light, without existence. The earth without existence. Gone or never was. Gone...

... When the door opened I almost smiled from the narrow bed where I sat against the wall with my knees up.

Dog motioned with the .357 magnum. I got up and walked out of the dark room ahead of him.

THIRTY-NINE

DOG PRODDED ME down the stairs to the entry room with the business counter, the rows of brass hooks for room keys, and the benches where the ladies had waited in their dazzling underwear for the muddy miners and horse-stinking cowhands. A different music came through the archway from the public waiting room.

"Inside."

The music still came from Jasper Murdoch's portable stereo tape deck, and the small leader of the kidnappers sat on the same wine velvet couch where I had last faced him. The smashed lamps still lay strewn across the polished floor in their separate corners. But the music was dance music, disco and the nostalgia of the fifties and sixties, and Murdoch was no longer alone in the big room, bright now with the brilliance of crystal chandeliers that had once held candles. The Indian, Charley, sucked his beer can on a couch and rocked his squat body to the disco beat as if in a trance. Where space had been cleared, Alan and Helen Kay Campbell danced.

"Fortune!" Jasper Murdoch waved a bottle. "It's a party! Dog, give the man a drink."

Dog handed me a can of beer from a large plastic cooler full of ice set on the floor of the elegant old room. For the party, he wore a blazing red jump suit.

"Food on the table!" Murdoch aimed the colorless bottle at a round coffee table of cold meats, cheese, bread, and
liquor bottles. "A party for our guests, right?"

Alan and Helen Kay danced to the heavy rhythm of a late
rock song of the early sixties. They had not seemed surprised to see me, danced without looking at me. Awkward
dancing, stiff and nervous.

"Tomorrow we get rich and everyone goes home! Today
we party! The way it's supposed to be!"

The Indian began to chant a monotone of some ancient
desert ritual. Alan Campbell danced with a can of beer
against Helen Kay's back. She drank from a glass of brown
liquid as they danced past a table, wore a white evening
party dress as elegant as her model's face and figure. She
didn't dance like a model, and who had given her the dress?
Dog drank cognac from an expensive bottle. Only the best
for King Dog.

"Fun and party! The only way to go, right, Dog man?
Wine and women. Tomorrow's coming!"

Murdoch was drunk and swaying on the velvet couch. For
the first time not in control, uncertainty in his hooded eyes.
The Indian chanted the endless magic of a forgotten time.
Alan Campbell danced and whispered, his face sweating in
the cool mountain night. Helen Kay, awkward in the white
dress, danced stiffly to the slow ballads of the sixties, ballads of leaving and wandering alone because the price of
love was being in one place and that was too high. Murdoch tilted his colorless bottle, drank.

"Fortune needs a dance! Charley, get your woman to
dance with Fortune!"

Dog, silent against a wall, tasted his cognac lightly, appreciated the best, and watched Murdoch.

"You're drunk, Charley! A drunken Indian! Very bad!
No woman for a drunken Indian! Dog, get Charley's
woman!"

Dog went. The Indian chanted his magic monotone. Alan and Helen Kay danced. Nervous and watchful. Afraid. But of what? They didn't act like kidnap victims, yet not like partners in extortion either. Not like captives, yet somehow prisoners. Not looking for escape, as if escape made no difference, yet scared. Nervous. Waiting for something.

Murdoch waved the unlabeled bottle. Mescal, maybe, from over the border. Unlabeled, untaxed, and lethal.

"Make your own rules! Your own game. They make their rules for their game so they got to win. What's in it for us? Nothing. Their rules for themselves and the rest of us are out!"

Dog returned. The short Indian woman with him was dressed in layers of long, heavy colored skirts and shawls, moccasins barely visible, black hair in a single braid, silver on her arms and in her ears, black eyes. Old clothes and a young face. Very young, a girl. Dog pushed her to me.

"Dance."

At least it was a ballad. The Indian girl looked at my missing arm, and then down at my feet, and did the leading. She had learned dancing that wasn't Indian. Dog went back to his wall, to his cognac bottle, and to watching Jasper Murdoch.

"Reservations and welfare. The price they pay to keep the Indians and blacks and dirt poor and freaks out of their game. Yessir! You better believe it." He drank, stared at nothing.

Helen Kay and Alan stopped dancing, sat down. They began to make sandwiches from the meat and cheese and bread. A gray cat appeared to watch them. Alan gave the cat a piece of ham. Dog looked at Alan and Helen Kay, and then looked at the cat.

Murdoch drank. "You get born, you get sold. The other guy's game. A bill of goods, a snipe hunt."

I stopped dancing. The Indian girl moved silently to the Indian, Charley. His chant was almost inaudible now. Alan and Helen Kay ate their sandwiches and looked toward me as I sat down and made one for myself. Dog watched the gray cat. The cat jumped lightly onto the food table.

Murdoch drank. "Criminals. Outlaws. That's what we are."

Helen Kay moved her head, her eyes fixed on me. A faint motion of complicity, of conspiracy, as if we had something to share. Maybe we did. Alan Campbell moved nervously. The Indian had the Indian girl beside him. Murdoch drank. The gray cat caught a piece of ham in its teeth, shook the ham like a mouse. Dog drew his gun from somewhere under the red jump suit and shot at the cat. The cat snarled and vanished under a couch. Dog walked to the food table, threw a piece of ham out onto the floor.

"In the jungle, not the town." Murdoch spoke, drank. "No walls and no rules. Free in the jungle. Hunted not caged."

Dog threw a piece of salami. The cat's head appeared from under the couch. Helen Kay looked at me. I nodded. The cat crept out and moved toward the meat on the floor. It had almost reached the meat when Dog fired and blew it into bloody pieces. Blood and fur and flesh dripped from the velvet couches and polished mahogany where the girls and miners had sat long ago.

"The tiger," Murdoch said, "not the fucking sheep."

The Indian closed his eyes and took up his medicine chant. The Indian girl watched Dog as he put away his gun. Murdoch laid his head down on the couch and went to sleep. The bottle dropped from his hand, rolled spilling. The Indian girl said something low. The Indian stood, picked up Murdoch, carried him out of the room. No one touched the spilling bottle or the remains of the slaughtered cat.

"Party's over," Dog said.

FORTY

N THE SMALL second-floor room with the mountain night
nd the snow outside I sat on the narrow bed in the dark.
'he noises of the restored old bordello disappeared one by
ne: distant footsteps; coughing; water in a sink; the flush
f a toilet. Until there was only the wind and the creaking
f old boards.

I sat on the narrow bed. I would not sleep tonight.

Only wait. The final helplessness—to wait and not know
or what or when. Hope or pain, life or death. Without
ower to change a degree or a second of what it would be,
r to even know what it would be or when. No longer hu-
aan.

I would not sleep. But the body doesn't give a damn about
vhat you want to do, and I came awake with a jerk to the
ound of the key turning in the lock. The sound of the
wentieth century. A shadow entered from the corridor that
vas as dark now as the room. A shadow in ghostly white.

"Fortune?"

Helen Kay. She stood over the bed, slim in the party dress.

"They're all asleep. Jasper and the Indian are passed out
runk, but we had to wait for Dog. The black bastard never
oes to bed. Listen, we—"

"Dog's in bed now?"

"In his room. Alan's down there watching. Listen, For-
une, you've got to get away and get help. We tried to find
our car but we couldn't. You'll have to walk out to the
ighway. There's a gas station two miles up the highway to-
ard Flagstaff, you can call the sheriff from there."

"For what, a ride?"

"To tell him to come up here and stop Jasper!"

"Stop him from what?" I said. "You weren't kid
napped. He's your brother. In the family."

I sensed her shaking her head violently, a movement o
the darkness itself. "He found us in New York and made u
go along with the scam! He didn't give a damn about u
taking off out of Chatham until goddamn Ian Campbel
called him looking for us. That's when he got the kidnap
ping idea, why not make Campbell pay if he wanted u
back!"

"How did he make you play along?"

"You don't understand! You don't know him!" I hear
a desperation in her voice, even terror. "They didn't ask u
to do it, they told us. We had no choice. If we tried to cros
J.J. he'd kill us, you don't know him! We're prisoners a
much as you! More! J.J. don't give a shit about me, an
Alan's nothing to him. That Dog King'd kill anyone for
dime with five cents' change! You got to get away and brin
the cops!"

"Why try to cross him at all? Why not just go along, tak
your cut? Who'd have known if you hadn't just told me
Why turn me loose, make trouble for them?"

I could see her now, nervous and biting a knuckle. He
almost classically beautiful face and body, and the incon
gruous gutter voice and manner. Her face not only anxiou
now, urgent.

"No way, you hear? We go along, what happens after h
got the cash in his fist? You can't trust him! I mean, he'
crazy. Maybe he pays us, maybe he kills us! You got to g
get help!"

There was a certain truth to what she was telling me. If
was in their place I'd worry a lot about Murdoch and Dog
But there had to be something else. Not just the danger of
violent and unpredictable brother. Possible danger is on
thing; certain danger is another. She wasn't the kind t
worry about possible danger, to be afraid of tomorrow

Heedless of anything but the immediate moment. There had to be a danger she knew now. Somehow, she knew they were in violent danger—or would be soon.

"What do you know I don't?"

"Nothing!" she cried, whispering it in the dark room. "You got to hurry, Fortune! They could wake up anytime."

"Why me? Why not run yourselves? You're loose."

She shook her head. "If we double-crossed him he'd go crazy and kill us for sure, hunt us down. If we run they'll get away from the cops, 'n' they'd get us no matter what. Anyway, we ain't got clothes for the snow. You do, you can get the sheriff!"

"They'll know you let me out of the room."

"No they won't! All the keys fit all the locks. This is an old whorehouse, you know? We'll have our key, they'll figure you found one in the room."

I wondered if it showed how reckless she was, or devious, or just desperate. So scared she'd take any risk to get me to bring the sheriff, or really believed it would work, or had some scheme up her sleeve she wasn't telling me? It didn't matter. I could escape and save myself, but that wouldn't help Alan and Helen Kay. My job was to bring them back to Ian Campbell, and saving myself wouldn't do that. I could bring the sheriff, but if I did that there was a good chance Alan and Helen Kay would be dead when we got here.

Alan Campbell came into the dark room. "What the hell's going on," he whispered. "He's got to hurry!"

"No, I don't," I said. "I'm not going."

They stared at me in the dark room.

"If I brought the sheriff now there's a good chance that when we got here we wouldn't find them here or you two alive. They'll know you let me out no matter what you hope, and even if they don't it's odds-on they'd spot the sheriff coming in and you'd be dead and they'd be gone when we reached the valley."

They stared at each other.

"The best way," I said, "is to go along with the ransom plan and hope we find an angle before the cash changes hands. If not, it's better to pay up and make sure you two are safe. Unless you know something I don't."

"No," Helen Kay said, "there ain't nothing."

I could slip down the stairs now and out and run all the way down to the highway and get away. It would be good to do that. I wanted to do that. But I had a job, work to do, and in the end that was all I did have. My work.

"Your brother," I said to Helen Kay where she stood close to Alan Campbell in her white dress in the dark room, "he talks as if he lost something, as if he wants something he can't have. What is it? What made him the way he is?"

"He can't make it."

"Make it?"

"With girls, women. He can't get it up." She laughed. "He got no balls, or something. I never looked, you know?"

"How long has he been that way?"

"Since that bear got him that time. Maybe around twelve."

"Who else knows?"

"I don't know, not too many people. Some of the girls. He used to date my girl friends, then they'd find out and dump him."

"The damned queer!" Alan Campbell said. "And he acts so tough!"

Helen Kay said, "Don't you ever call him a queer or you'll find out how tough he really is. Jesus!"

"He still goes out with women?" I said.

She shook her head. "Nah, not for a long time. I mean, why would he, he can't do nothing. And who'd go out with him after a couple of times?"

"Where's his room?" I asked.

Somehow, I had the feeling of getting near to the solution of one of my problems.

"You mean his room here?" Helen Kay said.

"Here."

"Up on the third floor. He likes the view of the damned valley, I guess. You can't go up there! Besides, he keeps it locked, I never been in it."

"You said all the keys fit all the doors. I'll take your key."

"You're as crazy as he is! You'll get us all killed!"

"He's drunk and asleep. Give me your key and go back to your room. Where is it?"

"Down the hall, last on the left."

"I'll lock this door in case Dog checks. When I'm through, I'll give you your key back, and you can lock me in my room."

She gave me her key. She wasn't happy. Neither was Alan Campbell, but they went back to their room, and I went slowly up the dark stairs of the creaking old bordello to the third floor. This was where the girls would have lived and slept alone, and the rooms were a lot smaller. I listened at the door of Murdoch's room for a time. There was the faint sound of snoring. I used Helen Kay's key. It worked. As I slipped inside I wondered why Jasper Murdoch would lock his door; what did he have to be afraid of here in his remote mountain valley?

A small light was on in the low room under the eaves. Murdoch was scared of the dark. He lay sprawled supine on a narrow cot still wearing his planter's white tropical suit. The low, rattling snore of a drunk. And I saw why he locked his door. Why it was always locked. I saw the women.

They were pasted all over the ceiling and every wall.
Women. Endless, overlapping, blending. Photographs and
clippings of the faces, the bodies, the lips, the smiles of
women. Women in all shapes, all colors, all sizes. Dressed
from head to toe in robes and furs, and naked. In uni-
forms. On beds. In garter belts. In leather and in rubber
boots and aprons. In nightgowns. A hundred different
nightgowns. Glossy photos from the pornographers of the
world, and glossy publicity shots of a thousand eager star-
lets. Famous women clipped from every imaginable magazine, and nameless women from every other magazine. Rita
Hayworth in her famous kneeling nightgown pose from
World War II. Monroe on her red velvet. Naked center-
folds and overdressed fashion ladies. High school girls and
college girls, cheerleaders and athletes. And local girls.

She smiled straight at me. Younger, dressed in the sweater
of a high school girl. With Helen Kay among a group of
cheerleaders. Dancing at some formal dance. Sitting in
someone's car, her legs dangling out up to the thighs,
laughing. The winner of a beauty contest. At the table in
some local Flagstaff bar. In a production of *Fiddler on the
Roof*, the sad, youngest daughter. In some more professional production of *Barefoot in the Park*. As Joan of Arc.
In another beauty contest. All centered around what had to
be her high school senior portrait.

Sarah Borden.

A girl who had a need to keep anyone she had ever had,
who wanted everyone she had ever known to love her, who
never let go of even those she abandoned.

I left Jasper Murdoch still sleeping, went down and got
Helen Kay to lock me back in my room, and lay down on the
cot to get what sleep I could before morning.

FORTY-ONE

I WOKE UP TO the leitmotif of the twentieth century—a key turning in my lock. The Indian stood in the doorway. He had no gun. I didn't ask what weapon he had. I didn't really want to know.

He took me down some back stairs into a large kitchen. The morning outside the windows was gray with a thick fog low on the mountains. Jasper Murdoch sat at the kitchen table in the cowboy outfit Leah Aherne had seen outside the Hotel Emerson back in New York: black Stetson, decorated shirt with string tie, silver-decorated leather vest, boot jeans, and snakeskin western boots. Mahler was on the stereo again, the unfinished Tenth Symphony, and the small man showed no signs of his drinking. He motioned to a pot of coffee and a brown bag of doughnuts.

"Eat."

I poured a cup of coffee. Alan and Helen Kay sat together near an electric heater. Dog sharpened a long, thin knife near a window that looked out across the valley and the snow to the fog low on the slopes. Murdoch warmed his hands over his cup of coffee, listened to his reconstructed Mahler Tenth.

"Campbell wants to see 'em," Murdoch said. "Flaco is on the way up with him to meet us. You'll fix the payoff." He listened to the music. A bass drum was booming out slow, spaced strokes of doom. "A funeral. His own funeral."

"How do I fix the payoff?"

"We tell you later."

"Tell me about Sarah Borden."

"Sarah?" He blinked as the bass drum boomed out it:
fate. "Always liked Sarah. She's a big actress now. In New
York." He seemed to think, then shook his head and ate a
doughnut.

Like all the half sane, he was two people, maybe more.
Part of him still lived in the "real" world, wanted it. Par:
of him hated that world, had chosen his violent anti-world,
yet rejected that violence and anger too. So he hid inside,
with his unseen voices and his music, and shaped a third
world where he was neither rejected nor guilty.

"Charley's ready," Dog said at the kitchen window.

Half crazy too, Dog, but for him there was only the one
world. His world. Synthesized from his rejection and his
need, one simple world where nothing existed except himself. Neither morality nor immorality, the only value himself. A universe of one, in which all else—people, places,
things—were only tools for his benefit. Everything deter-
mined entirely by its relation to Dog King and what Dog
King wanted at any given moment. Nothing fixed or absolute except himself.

"Let's go then," Jasper Murdoch said.

He picked up the custom-made stereo tape deck and we
all walked out into the chill of the mountain morning with
its snow and the fog just above the tops of the pines. The
Indian stood between my Jeep and an old blue Cadillac. He
got into the Caddy with Jasper Murdoch and Helen Kay.
Dog motioned me behind the wheel of my Jeep, put Alan in
the front seat beside me, and got into the back himself.

"Right out the way you come in," he said to me.

I drove down the dirt road with the old Caddy behind.
The dark, running creek seemed more menacing in the
drifting fog as it cut swift between the banks of snow and
around the Boot Hill bluff. The drive down through the
steep canyons under the dark trees was less beautiful than

the trip up had been. Or maybe that was only Dog and his knife behind me.

"Right," Dog said when we reached the county highway.

I drove south to I-4, skirted Flagstaff to Alternate 89, went south for a mile or two and into a narrow side road just north of Oak Creek Canyon. A half a mile on into the pines a clearing opened to the left in a pale sunlight breaking now through the mountain fog. The red Lincoln limousine stood in the clearing, a skinny old man in black beside the front door: Flaco Sanchez, the fourth member of the gang.

"Turn in here and stop," Dog instructed.

We were still a hundred feet from the red limousine. Ian Campbell got out of the back seat of the limo. His lean face was tight and anxious. A nervous, worried father. Alan didn't see him, was looking back to where the old Caddy pulled up behind us and Murdoch and Helen Kay got out. Ian Campbell began to walk.

"Stay right over there, big man," Dog said.

He prodded Alan out of the Jeep with his knife. Helen Kay and Murdoch joined us. There was a silence in the clearing as the thin morning sun filtered through the tall pines. I felt as if we were in one of those spy movies where two sides meet across a no-man's land to exchange captured agents and everyone is tense and nervous, all hands on triggers and suspicious eyes alert.

"Here they are, Campbell," Murdoch said. "Alive."

Across the clearing Ian Campbell stared toward us. At Alan and Helen Kay and Murdoch and Dog and me. I saw the change in his face. In his eyes and his face. A sudden... what? Fear? Shock? Because he'd never seen Jasper Murdoch and Dog, never really believed the danger to Alan? Now suddenly faced it? A kind of disbelief as he stared toward us. Confusion. Because I was there? Shocked to see me there on the other side?

I called out, "They caught me snooping around."

"Trying to save you your beautiful money," Jasper Murdoch said. He still carried the portable stereo, Sibelius playing now under the pines. "Is that it, Campbell? Can we do business?"

"Fortune," Campbell said, called, stared toward us. "You...I...what?..."

Helen Kay began to shout, "Do what they want, Mr. Campbell! They'll kill us if you don't! We know too much! We can tell everyone too much!"

"Dad!" Alan called. "We'll give back everything we ran off with! We promise! Just pay them, Dad, and we'll make it up to you, do everything you want from us!"

"He's my brother," Helen Kay cried, "but he'll kill us and take everything!"

"Dad!" Alan called. "You got to—!"

Dog jabbed Alan lightly with his knife.

"The man got the idea," Dog said.

Across the distance of thin mountain morning sunlight, Ian Campbell stood and went on staring at his son, at Helen Kay, at Jasper Murdoch, and at me. He licked his lips. Then nodded.

"What do I do now?" His voice was thick. He cleared his throat. "I mean, where do we make the trade?"

Murdoch took my arm. "You and Fortune'll drive out of here. You get the money, then Fortune brings you out to our camp. He knows there's no way anyone gets in there without us spotting them, you understand?"

Dog said, "We see cops, troops, anythin' out of line they're dead. They're dead and we're gone. Fortune knows."

He prodded me back into my Jeep, Murdoch signaled the skinny driver, Flaco Sanchez. The old border outlaw got into the limo, drove it up to us. Alan and Dog got in, Murdoch and Helen Kay returned to the old Caddy, and they drove away. Alone in the clearing, Ian Campbell walked slowly toward me and the Jeep. He got in and I drove off.

"What was scaring you back there? A shock?"

He shook his head. "I don't know what you mean. Nothing scared me back there."

"Confused you."

"Nothing confused me," he said. "Can we get to the motel?"

We drove north to Flagstaff, and south again on I-17 toward Camp Verde. What was it? Ian Campbell scared the moment he saw us, almost stunned. Alan and Helen Kay terrified of more than some possible danger after the payoff. I didn't know, then all at once I did. I thought I did. As we drove on south in the warming morning sun I went back over the whole thing in my mind from the first day and I knew what was terrifying Alan and Helen Kay, what Ian Campbell had seen there in the clearing.

FORTY-TWO

CAMPBELL'S RENTED Ford was the only car parked in front of his unit at the Desert Wind Motel in Camp Verde. Steve Norris wasn't there.

"Where is he?" I asked Campbell.

"At another motel down in Phoenix. I thought it best to keep the money a long way from them while they had me too."

In the motel room he stretched out on the bed, his hands behind his head, his eyes up toward the ceiling.

"You better get him up here with the money. It gets dark early in these mountains, we should leave as soon as I get back."

"Where are you going?"

"On some business."

I waited for him to tell me that the only business I had
now was his business, but he said nothing. Only stared up
at the motel-room ceiling. There was something very much
on his mind. Something heavy.

Outside I got back into my rented Jeep and drove north
to Flagstaff once more. I located Dr. Benjamin De Mott,
D.D.S., at number 14 Winslow Street. It was a large frame
house with his dentist office at the rear. I showed De Mott
the appointment card I'd found in Alan and Helen Kay's
house in Chatham.

"It's one of mine, yes," the doctor said.

He was a large, jolly-looking man who probably hated to
hurt his patients. I showed him my picture of Alan Campbell.

"Was this the man you gave that card to?"

He took the card. "He looks familiar. Let me call my re-
ceptionist."

She was a young girl. "Sure, a three-session root canal.
That was the last session and he never paid us! Eddie
McBride."

"You're sure?"

"That was his name. I keep a list of deadbeats."

"McBride, yes," De Mott said. "Talked about motorcycles."

I thanked them, went back to the Jeep. No one had told
me that Alan Campbell had been in Flagstaff this summer.
Only two months before Ian Campbell went to Europe with
Leah Aherne, and under a different name.

I made one more stop before driving back south to Camp
Verde and the Desert Wind Motel.

FORTY-THREE

ANOTHER FORD was parked behind Ian Campbell's rental at the Desert Wind. As I went in Steve Norris looked up from where he sat with an attaché case in his lap. He wore hiking boots and hunting clothes, a pile-lined parka on the back of his chair.

"Ready for action?" I said.

"For anything I can do," Norris said.

Ian Campbell was still on the bed looking at the ceiling.

"Do we go now? It's getting late."

"You better get a coat and overshoes," I told him.

He sat up, stood. "I've got a coat, the hell with the over-shoes. I want to get this done. Norris has the money."

"Do you have a gun?"

Norris produced a snub-nosed .38 Colt.

"Guns?" Campbell said. "Will they like that, Fortune?"

"They won't know."

"I don't have one anyway."

"There's a rifle in the Jeep. Can you shoot?"

"I've shot. Can we go now?"

In the rented Jeep we drove north to Flagstaff and on along the county highway to the turnoff into Little Chee Canyon. Under the thick pines, Ian Campbell tapped his foot beside me as I drove up the twisting road above the dark, rushing creek toward High Point Camp. Norris rode in the back. The afternoon mountain sunlight came to meet us as we emerged from the trees into the high valley. I drove around the bluff below Boot Hill. As soon as the restored old bordello was in sight up against the mountain, I stopped and turned the Jeep facing back the way we had come.

Campbell looked around. "Where are they? Why stop here?"

"They're in that big building up on the slope. Some of them are watching the road. We're stopping here because it's time to talk before they come down and before they spot the sheriff."

"The sheriff?" Norris said.

"He's bringing his men around through the woods the long way. He thinks he can get close without being seen. I worked it out with him before I came back to the Desert Wind."

"They'll kill them!" Campbell was white.

I looked at him. "Why do you care?"

"I'll warn them!" Campbell started to get out of the Jeep. "I tell them, maybe they won't kill them!"

I said, "What do you care if they do, Campbell?"

"Christ, Fortune," Norris swore, "that's Alan in there, that's his son!"

"No," I said. "No, that's not Alan Campbell up there. That's not his son, and he knows it. He knew it the moment he saw them in that clearing earlier today."

Campbell was staring up the slope to where they had all come out of the old bordello. Murdoch was with Helen Kay and whoever it was pretending to be Alan Campbell. Dog and the Indian, Charley, walked on either side with their guns. The red Lincoln limousine was on the driveway down to the road behind them. I expected the driver, Flaco, would be armed too. Who was watching the road in?

Campbell walked toward them. "I'll tell them!"

"You better not," I said. "Murdoch doesn't know, none of them do except Helen Kay, and you don't want them to find out."

Campbell stopped, licked his lips, stared upward.

Norris said, "You're sure, Fortune? That's not Alan?"

"Was Alan out here in Flagstaff last summer? Was he ever out here?"

"Not that I know."

I said, "Campbell?"

Ian Campbell said nothing, stared up the slope.

I told Norris about Dr. De Mott. "He identified the photo of Alan as the man he worked on out here, but Alan's never been to Flagstaff. Helen Kay hasn't been back in three years." I looked up the slope to where they were walking down toward us now. Wary and alert, probably wondering why I had stopped so far from the bordello. It was a risk I had to take.

"I should have guessed sooner. I said it myself: 'They didn't want to be found, not by anyone from Chatham.' Sarah Borden said it, they weren't hiding from her, or from the people in Derry City. Only from anyone who knew Alan Campbell really well. Because whoever that is up there, in the right clothes and coached by Helen Kay, looks enough like Alan Campbell to pass with those who don't know him too well and in photographs supposed to be Alan. But not in person, moving and talking."

"But they went to Edna! To his mother!"

"Who hadn't seen him for ten years. A woman who thinks of just about nothing except herself. No, I should have seen it right off. They weren't hiding from anyone except those from Chatham. They pulled their trick on me, and ran, only after I told them *you* were with me, Norris. When I found them, Alan's manner was all wrong—not unconfident, not shy. At Computer Methods Alan never spoke of going away, selling his house. Leah Aherne's description of Alan didn't come near the Alan I met. He didn't quit the company in person, and Helen Kay picked up his money.

"It all pointed to someone who wasn't Alan even *before* they left Chatham. The motor oil in the bedroom. Some-

one parked a motorcycle in their bedroom, and that wasn't
the Alan Campbell I'd been told about. Alan hated speed,
hated machines. In Derry City this time Alan wasn't jealous, got as wild and drunk as Helen Kay, and that wasn't
like Alan Campbell. I think they went to Derry City to see
if the fake Alan could pass, so whoever he is he'd become
Alan even before September."

I looked up the slope again to where the fake Alan walked
beside Helen Kay. Neither of them looked happy.

"Where is Alan, then?" Norris said.

"Yeh," I said, "where is Alan?"

Campbell still stood out in front of the Jeep. Sweat
beaded his face, his hands opened and closed spasmodi-
cally.

"Don't you give a damn where Alan is?" I said. "If he's
alive or dead? What the hell's so important you don't even
have time to care if your son's alive or dead?"

He just stood there in the afternoon mountain sun.

"You want something Alan and Helen Kay took with
them when they ran off, whoever Alan really is. That's all
that makes any sense. That's what was happening in the
clearing this morning. You knew it wasn't Alan, and they
knew you knew, and they were telling you that if you kept
quiet and ransomed them they'd give you back what they
took."

Campbell turned, came back. "All right, yes! They've got
what I want but I have to ransom them. The kidnappers
don't know about Alan or the letter! If I ransom them, I get
the letter!"

So there it was. What Campbell had really wanted, what
had happened in the clearing, what Helen Kay was so terrified over. If I'd lied to Jasper Murdoch and Dog King
held out on them, I'd be scared too.

"What letter, Ian?" Norris said.

"Worth a quarter of a million dollars?" I said.

Campbell shook his head. "That's my business. We give
them the money, I get the letter, then we worry about Alan."

Norris said, "That's why you forced Turk Aherne out!
You've got some crooked deal—"

"Later, Norris," I said.

They were getting too close if we were to have any chance
of escaping without getting shot to hell if something went
wrong before or after the sheriff and his men arrived. Norris stared.

"My God," he said, "you're right. That's not Alan!"

"Show them the guns," I said. "Hold their attention."

I took out my old cannon. Norris showed his .38 Colt.
Campbell took the rifle from the Jeep. On the slope they all
stopped. Jasper Murdoch, Dog, and the Indian watched us.

"What you figure on doin' with those?" Dog called.

Jasper Murdoch said, "What are the guns for, Fortune?"

"Comfort," I said. "I feel a lot more comfortable. We
won't use them unless you try something. We're not killers."

"We are," Murdoch said. "That's the edge. Do we deal
or start a war?"

Campbell held out the attaché case. "I've got the money."

"Swell," Murdoch said. "Just bring—"

Norris stood up behind me. I turned too late.

"No!" Norris shouted. "He's not going to pay you!
Maybe that's your sister, but that guy's not Alan Campbell. Where is Alan Campbell, you hear? Tell us what's
happened to Alan!"

On the rutted road and the snow-covered slope we froze
as rigid as our own long shadows in the late afternoon sun.
A mountain wind was beginning to move the tall pines on
the high slopes, rattle the loose boards in the ruined old
buildings on the banks of the dark, swiftly moving creek. It
was Dog who spoke first.

"What the fuck's the cat talking about, J.J.?"

Jasper Murdoch looked toward me. "Fortune?"

"No," I said, "he's not Alan Campbell. Almost a twin, but he's not Alan."

Helen Kay stepped quickly toward her brother, faced the small, pale man on the mountain slope in the rising wind. A desperation in her voice.

"Jasper, listen! He'll pay!" Watching Dog and the Indian out of the corner of her eye, facing Jasper Murdoch. "We've got something better than his goddamned son, something he wants more! He knew about Alan as soon as he saw us this morning, but he's here anyway! He'll pay, I swear!" She reached into the pocket of the motorcycle jacket she wore now and pulled out an envelope. "Look, it's a letter he got from some government guy telling all about a bribe Campbell paid the guy to get a big government contract for his company, then they'd overcharge the government with the government guy okaying all the phony charges! It's all right, in the letter: names; dates; what and how and when and how much! We didn't mean to fool you, Jasper! You just grabbed us in New York, and wanted to hold Alan for ransom, and I was scared to tell you he wasn't Alan, and then I was even more scared to tell you later. Look, he knew it wasn't his kid and he still came here with the money! He'll pay, I swear!"

Jasper Murdoch only stood there and stared at her. The fake Alan smiled around at everyone. The Indian leaned against a tree to my left, his .45 automatic aimed in the general direction of our Jeep. In the limousine up the road, the driver, Flaco Sanchez, sat with his hands out of sight. Dog spoke to Murdoch.

"The man's here," he said. "Guess he wants that letter."

Helen Kay's hands shook. "We was gonna tell you, swear!"

"Not your husband?" Murdoch said. He sounded almost shocked. In the same bedroom, and not her husband.

"Maybe the big man wants it so bad he pays more," Dog said.

Campbell moved a step up the slope with the attaché case. "A quarter of a million, not a penny more. And if anyone sees the letter, nothing. You get the money, I get the letter in my hand. Fortune and Norris don't touch it."

Murdoch said, "You lied to me."

"Okay," Dog said. "We ain't greedy, and I figure to handle Fortune and the other dude. Girl, walk on down the hill. Big man, you start up."

Murdoch looked toward Dog. "She fooled us, held out on us. She didn't tell us about her husband or the letter."

"It's a lousy world, J.J.," Dog said. "Ain't a lot o' folks honest like us. Straight-out mean and no good."

Helen Kay came down the slope toward us. Ian Campbell went up across the snow with the attaché case. When they were some ten yards apart, Dog called out to them:

"Okay, both of you put it on the ground right there."

Helen Kay placed the envelope on a rock. Ian Campbell set the money case into the snow.

"Now fetch," Dog called. "Grab your loot and head for home."

Campbell and Helen Kay passed each other without a single glance. Campbell put the letter in his pocket, came back toward the Jeep. Helen Kay carried the bag of money up to where Jasper Murdoch and Dog waited with the fake Alan.

"She made fools of us, Dog," Murdoch said. "Fortune knew all about it. She lied to us. She conned us, Dog."

Helen Kay reached them. Murdoch took the bag of money from her. He shot her without taking the Colt Agent from his pocket. Alan Campbell, whoever he really was, jumped on Murdoch, grabbing for his gun. I started the

Jeep, slammed it into drive. Up the slope Dog pulled the fake Alan off Murdoch and shot him twice. I had the Jeep moving and Ian Campbell ran toward us. Norris hung on and shot up the slope at Dog and Murdoch.

"Ian!" he cried. "Come on!"

The Indian was running down the slope at us firing his .45 automatic. Across the snow Jasper Murdoch was down. Near us, Ian Campbell lay bleeding behind the Jeep.

"Fortune!" Norris yelled.

I stopped the Jeep. Norris jumped out and bent over Campbell. I blazed away at the Indian with my old cannon. Norris dragged Campbell into the Jeep. The letter fell out of his pocket. I dropped my old gun on the floor of the Jeep, grabbed the letter, shoved it into my pocket, gunned the Jeep away.

Far up the mountain near the trees the small Indian woman, girl, had appeared. She shouted something I couldn't understand.

"Cops!" Dog yelled.

The driver, Flaco Sanchez, ran from the limousine, shooting at us. Far up the mountain near the trees the Indian girl looked down to where the Indian, Charley, lay in the snow. The driver and Dog helped Jasper Murdoch toward the limousine. The Indian girl vanished into the trees high up.

I careened the Jeep down the dirt road and around the Boot Hill bluff. With the creek dark and swollen beside us, I drove for the cover of the trees ahead and the twisting road down out of the mountain valley. Uniformed men ran out of the trees. The sheriff stopped our Jeep.

"That's a damned slow climb. We heard shooting. Anyone hurt?"

"Campbell, Helen Kay, and her man, whatever his real name is," I said. "We've got Campbell, the other two are till back there. The Indian's shot, and I think Murdoch was hit."

"We got an ambulance down on the highway." The sheriff ran on behind his deputies, called back, "Send my vehicles up!"

I drove as fast as I could down the dark canyon road above the black, rushing creek. Ian Campbell lay unconscious across the rear seat, blood soaking his shirt and suit. When we reached the highway I told them to take their cars up. The ambulance took Campbell off to Flagstaff. I turned the Jeep and headed back for High Point Camp behind the sheriff's cars.

"You got the letter," Norris said.

"I got it."

"What are you going to do with it?"

"Turn it over to the sheriff. It's evidence."

"Why not hold onto it a while? It's evidence in New Jersey and New York too."

I watched the curving road and listened for any sounds of battle up above in the high mountain valley. I heard nothing. Norris watched me. Then he looked down at the dark creek.

"I didn't even know I was going to do it," he said. "I was sitting in the Jeep, and all of a sudden I hated it all. Those kidnappers and Ian. Helen Kay and that fake Alan and their schemes. I hated what Ian had done to Max Aherne and to Leah and to me! I hated what I'd done to myself. I hated that Ian didn't give a damn about Alan. I wanted to stop all the lying and cheating and getting away with everything!"

"Yeh," I said.

It's easy to tell ourselves all the noble reasons we have for injuring someone else. They could even be true, but now I had other things on my mind as I rounded the Boot Hill bluff. They had covered the body of the fake Alan, and three of them were carrying Helen Kay to a squad car. The

Indian, Charley, sat against the wall of the bordello, a bloody bandage on his leg. I never could shoot straight. Two deputies stood over him with their guns out. The sheriff himself was far up the dirt road where it went into the forest again on the other side of the valley. He nodded ahead as we reached him.

"The road goes on back down that way for maybe five miles and comes out on another county highway. I just sent a couple of cars after them, but my guess is they're gone. They know the mountains too damned well. Tell me what happened."

He listened to the whole story. The only part I left out was that I had the letter. The sheriff scowled at Norris when I told his part in the bloodbath. He lit a cigarette, smoked.

"The kid's dead. Helen Kay could make it. The Indian ain't going to walk good from now on, but he'll stand trial fine. With Jasper being her brother we won't get kidnapping, but we'll get extortion and conspiracy murder."

"New York and New Jersey could maybe get murder," I said. I told him about Andrew Katz, Mrs. Schott, and Sarah Borden. And about what I'd found in Jasper Murdoch's room in the bordello.

"Sarah?" The sheriff looked sick. "Christ, you never told me that, Fortune. You're sure? Murdoch?"

"Pretty sure. He must have run across her while he was chasing Helen Kay. She never let anyone go."

"She didn't know about Jasper?"

"It doesn't look like it."

The sheriff walked back along the road in the now low late-afternoon mountain sunlight. They took the body of the fake Alan to a squad car. If Helen Kay made it, she could tell us who he had been. If she didn't, we might never know.

"Maybe the deputies found them down the road," I said. "At least maybe where they went."

I drove in the other direction, the way Jasper Murdoch, Dog, and the driver had escaped. A twilight falling on the mountains.

FORTY-FOUR

I WOULD NEVER have seen it if the evening sun had been five minutes higher or lower. A sudden flash, there and gone as I drove past. I stopped, backed up slowly. The glint of reflected sun came again. Thinner now, the sun already almost too low through the pines in the fading mountain evening.

"Something's there," I said. "Off the road maybe fifty yards."

Norris said nothing. I got out of the Jeep.

"Take the rifle and keep me covered," I said.

Holding my old cannon, I walked toward the trees and bushes where I had seen the flash. The ground just off the road here was bare and rocky, scoured by the winds. The snow was still on the ground as I neared the thick line of bushes, and I saw tire tracks. Ahead, some trees had been knocked over, the bushes crushed. I went in among the trees. I saw it, the red Lincoln limousine, closed in by the trees and thick brush, its rear window facing the road fifty yards away.

"Don't move . . . Fortune. Just . . . stand."

Jasper Murdoch's voice, low and thick.

". . . tell him to get the sheriff . . . Flaco's hurt. You got to . . . help Flaco . . ."

I called back out to Norris, "It's the limo! The driver's hurt, bleeding. I'll help him, you go get the sheriff."

Norris was alarmed. "What about Dog and Murdoch?"

"I can't leave the driver, and you wouldn't make much difference if they come back. The sheriff will. Hurry up!"

I sensed Norris hesitating, held my breath. If he left, I was at Murdoch's mercy. If he stayed, came to help me, Murdoch would probably kill us both.

"Okay," Norris called. "Be back fast!"

I listened to the Jeep start and fade away back toward High Point Camp. I didn't know if I felt relieved or abandoned.

"Put the gun . . . down. . . . Get in."

I put my old cannon on the forest floor, walked to the shadowy limousine. The driver, Flaco Sanchez, was slumped over the wheel in the front seat and not moving. I got into the back, sat on the jump seat.

"I told Dog you was a good detective. The others went right on past."

He was huddled deep in the far corner breathing carefully. In the dim light inside the big car his pale eyes were bright, feverish. He held his Colt Agent aimed at me. The hand on the gun was bloody and there was blood all over his western shirt, the leather vest, the jeans, and the snakeskin boots.

"You're bad," I said. "You need a doctor, the hospital."

"No! . . . I don't . . . need . . . nothing . . . no more."

That thickness was in his voice as if his throat were full. When he tried to speak loudly, was agitated, he could barely get the words out. Only when he spoke softly, whispered, could he breathe cautiously and speak. He smiled in the dimness.

"I'm good, Fortune. Dog does good work. You can trust Dog."

"Dog shot you?"

I looked around. I didn't see the attaché case of money.

"I got winged, the car must've too. We lost power, just got it in here. Dog had the Caddy, saw his chance. Smart, the Dog. When you see the chance you get your partner and grab the cash before he gets you."

"Dog took the money?"

"That's what it's all about."

He coughed. Pain agonized on his face. The inward eyes were so far inside I could see only the shine of the surface.

"You have to have help." I started to get up.

The shot smashed the side window over my shoulder. I sat down. His thick whisper was almost happy.

"Dog give me all the help I need to get where I'm going. Maybe I'll take you with me, do you a favor."

"Don't do me a favor," I said.

I saw his teeth. "You want to help, find my stereo."

It was on the car floor at his feet. He looked at me and I knew he couldn't move. To move was to risk his last small hold. He was ready, but not yet, not this instant.

I picked up the tape stereo, pressed the "play" button. The music filled the small space inside the limousine. I turned the volume as loud as I dared. Maybe somebody would hear it, one of the deputies coming back. It should have been Mahler, a funeral march, but it wasn't. Shostakovich, the violent Seventh at war.

Murdoch closed his eyes. "Maybe it's all war, everything. Take and grab and kill. When I was a kid I had this foster father played classical music in his TV store all the time. I took to it. I was a lonely kid in a stinking world where nobody gave a shit if I lived or died and the music was somethin' I could feel. I could see the music. Like a movie in my head no matter how rotten it got, how many times I got kicked."

His eyes were closed, and I tensed, but the gun didn't waver, and he could hear any movement in the small interior.

"Change it . . . the green button."

I pressed the green button. Another Shostakovich. He sat there in the corner seeing those imagined movies.

"After the bear chewed me up it was the only thing kept me goin'. Music and reading. I was a freak, a castrate. I couldn't do nothin' with girls. Who wants to be friends with a guy can't make it with girls? Who wants a freak around? The girls laughed so the boys had to laugh too. I hated them, and when I got too much of being treated like some animal I'd go out and break windows, slash tires, even set fires! It made me feel good. Like the music. Music 'n' smashing, that's what I liked. Music and stealing. Music . . . and killing . . . things . . ."

His thick whisper broke. He breathed hard. He had to be slipping. When he knew it, felt it, that would be the danger.

"Change it! . . . I want to hear . . . it all before . . . it's over . . . Change it! . . . Go on!"

I pushed the green button and it was suddenly Carl Nielsen. The hammering side drum of his Fifth Symphony. I listened for any sound in the now dark night. There was nothing. Not even a bird, or the soft footfall of some nocturnal animal.

His thick whisper was calm again. "You treat a guy like a freak he'll be a freak. He got nothin' to do except go out and be a freak, get his kicks smashing everything he can't have, everyone who pushed him outside. You kick me out of your world, I got to make my own, and maybe it won't be a world you like. Change it!"

I hit the button. Beethoven. The big end of the Ninth.

"It's the only thing makes me cry, music," he whispered from the dark corner of the back seat. "When you're a kid you got such big ideas about all you're gonna do. Stupid dreams. We all got to reach for something we don't really know what the hell it is and we ain't ever gonna get it anyway 'cause it ain't there!'' His breathing was harsher. He waited. The thick whisper hoarser. ''When I hear the music it's almost possible, you know? Even for me. I'm almost possible. Almost possible I got a real life.''

He lay back in his dim corner. He didn't tell me to change the tape this time, but I pushed the button anyway. I got Vaughan Williams, the wraithlike end of the Sixth Symphony. In the corner he opened his eyes and listened, the gun wavered.

''The only wound gets worse all the time, every day. The only part of you you miss more every year. Every year, every month, every damned day it gets worse and worse, hurts more 'n' more. And nothin' you can do 'cept make them pay.''

''Sarah Borden,'' I said. ''You made her pay.''

The soft, eerie, whispering song of the Vaughan Williams flowed in the dark back seat of the limousine. Murdoch's thick whisper fell lower, almost inaudible.

''She came to town here late, she didn't know. I never even talked to her. I used to see her when Helen Kay brought her around, watch her in town, at the school. I got all the snaps of her I could find, cut stuff out of the papers about her, got pics from theater stuff she did. She moved away. That was even better, I could imagine it all. Then Helen Kay said she was in New York. I called. She was glad to hear from me. She remembered me. She wanted to see me!'' He licked at his lips as if they were as parched as the desert, his tongue barely moving, the hoarse whisper groping for words. ''She was in that bedroom. In that nightgown. That food and booze was ready for a big night. With me. For me. So…I tried. You hear…Fortune? I…*tried*! She…laughed at me. She…I shot her. I hit her. I shot her again…again. The broom handle. I…I tried, goddamn her…I *tried*….''

He began to choke, coughing on the blood in his throat. Blood spurted from somewhere. I saw the pain in his eyes and it wasn't all physical pain.

"Did Andrew Katz and Mrs. Schott laugh too?"

His breathing was growing shallow, irregular.

"It was Dog. The one in the food store tried for a piece in his drawer, the old woman wouldn't shut up. Dog don't like complications when he works."

His choking cough began again, the blood bubbling somewhere down in his chest. The gun shook in his hand, and he held onto a seat strap to steady himself.

"Let me get help, Murdoch," I said.

"No!" The pistol steadied in his bloody hand. "Change it."

I pushed the button. It was the Sibelius Second Symphony, that last movement where the horseman rides alone across the great empty landscape of snow and pines and frozen lakes to fade into a distant dot still riding toward the far horizon.

His whisper was almost gone. "I got to give Dog the time. Help him make it clean away. I got to hold you so Dog makes it."

I didn't tell him that keeping me wouldn't help Dog. The police were a lot closer to Dog than I was. He really knew that. We all have to think that we count, that we're doing something of value, that we make a difference.

"Fortune?"

I had to bend closer to hear.

"Let him go. He got the money. A quarter of a million big ones." His voice grew louder. "He got his balls . . . both his arms . . . he can . . . do something . . ."

For an instant he seemed to rise up out of the corner and glare at me. But it was only an illusion of his rising voice, and he was glaring not at me but at something far from me. With eyes that no longer saw.

The pistol fell to the carpeted floor of the limousine.

Slumped in the corner of the long seat he looked less than half his own small size, like a child curled in the dark corner of a closet, alone.

I picked up the pistol by its barrel, slipped it into one of the plastic evidence bags I carry. The bags impress the clients.

In the front seat I checked the driver, Flaco Sanchez. He was dead, had been for over an hour. I realized I'd never heard him speak.

I started to walk back along the dark road. It was growing cold. I was glad to see the lights coming toward me.

FORTY-FIVE

IT TOOK A LONG time to close it all out. Sheriff Gwynne had to tell Sarah Borden's parents what had happened to her. I didn't envy him. He sent Murdoch's .38 Colt Agent and a report to Captain Pearce in New York and closed that part of it.

I flew east to help search for Alan Campbell. Helen Kay was in the Flagstaff hospital's intensive care unit; they didn't know if she'd make it or not. Ian Campbell would be in the hospital at least five days with a deep scalp wound on his head and a clean shot through his left arm. So Steve Norris and I went east alone.

The Chatham Police and the New Jersey State Troopers met us. They'd already found Alan. Buried in a sand trap on the golf course just over the back fence from his house in Chatham.

"The yard was too hard to have anyone buried in it, hadn't been dug in for over a year," the state police officer said, "and we searched the house from top to bottom and found nothing. That was when Captain Ciardi there said look in the sand trap.''

"We had a case just like it about twelve years ago," the captain of the Chatham Police said. "I guess these murderers don't have a lot of imagination."

The coroner said that Alan had been dead since at least late August. He'd been killed by multiple blows to the head. He was wearing slacks, a sport shirt, and sandals, as if he'd been just relaxing at home when he died. Norris and Leah Aherne took charge of the body, and I went back to Flagstaff.

I found Ian Campbell walking around his hospital room with a bandage on his head and his arm in a sling and talking with his lawyer. I told him. It was the lawyer who paled.

"My God! Alan? Dead? What can I do, Ian?"

"You can call Edna," Ian Campbell said. "Tell her I'll arrange the funeral. If she wants to come she can stay at the house."

The lawyer looked green as he went out. A corporation lawyer, not used to violence. Campbell stood at his window that overlooked the snow streets of Flagstaff. He seemed to be watching the people pass as if it was wrong that they should be walking down there, free and unhurt.

"It's been quite a week," he said. "Lost my big chance, maybe my company, now my son."

"In that order?" I said.

He turned. "All right, Fortune, you don't like me. I'm sorry. I'm sorry my son is dead. But I'm a lot sorrier that I've lost all my plans because I had a son who couldn't handle women so had to marry a girl who was little more than a wild animal, and with an insane brother, just because she was the first woman who ever said yes to him!" He turned back to the window. "I had it all in my hands, and now it's gone."

"Yeh," I said to his back, "you had it all: family, looks, brains, education, the right social standing, everything. Too bad you couldn't think of more to do with it than grab at a few small-time dollars."

He said nothing to that. I went to the door.

"Fortune?" He didn't turn at the window. "Steve Norris says you picked up the letter. You have it?"

I considered his back for a time. "It's evidence in a kidnapping, an extortion, and four or five murders depending on how you look at Jasper Murdoch's shooting. It'll have to go into the record."

"I see."

I waited, but that was all he said. I turned back to the door.

"I'll send my bill."

"You don't really expect me to pay you?"

"Not really," I said.

He had other sons but only one business to make him important. By his own standards he'd been almost on top, and in a way I felt sorry for him, but he'd come out all right. It was to no one's advantage to send him to jail or destroy Computer Methods Corporation. He'd apologize, pay a stiff fine, let Max Aherne run the company, and wait to try again. Politics was probably over, but you never knew. Crimes don't seem to matter these days if enough people like you because you think the way they want you to think.

I stopped to tell Sheriff Gwynne about Alan Campbell, but he already knew. The New Jersey authorities had started extradition on Helen Kay for as soon as she could travel. In Flagstaff they'd already charged the Indian, Charley, with extortion and conspiracy to murder. The two other New Jersey murders would have to wait for Dog King's capture. He was still running unseen with Ian Campbell's quarter of a million, and from time to time on my flight home I found myself hoping he'd get clean away with the cash, beat the game. We're a strange species.

In my office/apartment I showered, shaved, and called Kay Michaels. I hoped she hadn't gone back to California yet. She hadn't. We had dinner. And drinks. And later, in the dark of my narrow one-room loft with its ancient brass bed I told her about the whole case.

"Sarah Borden must have recognized Jasper Murdoch when I described him that night in Downey's. His being in town, a man from home, would have intrigued her, and she had no reason to let me know she knew him."

"Sure she could handle anyone. Damn fool girl."

"Helen Kay recognized Jasper's description right away, of course, knew he was looking for her but didn't know why then. They acted odd when I talked about murder because they thought we'd found Alan. When they realized that we hadn't, they were relieved as hell. I missed that."

"Why did they kill him, Dan?"

"She told me in that first hotel, she just didn't mention they'd killed Alan. Chatham had become a royal drag. She hated Ian being around all the time, hanging over their lives, controlling them or trying to. She wanted a new man, a new place."

"But why murder the boy?"

"Money. They probably only got the idea after she'd taken up with the fake Alan and realized how much alike he and Alan looked. I expect they'd known each other at least casually in Flagstaff, and she might have remembered his resemblance to Alan, but I doubt it. Just chance."

In the morning I took her to Kennedy. I asked her to come back soon and stay longer. She asked me to come to California and stay for good. I said I'd think about it. I will. The violent and the indifferent are taking my city away.

They buried Alan Campbell in Chatham. Everyone was there except Alan's mother. She sent flowers, but she wasn't a woman who could face funerals.

Helen Kay was brought back from Flagstaff. She told them all to go to hell, blamed everything on the dead fake Alan.

I took the Erie Lackawanna out to Chatham once more. They had Helen Kay in a guarded room in a hospital down in Summit. She took one look at me, said, "Shit," and turned away.

I said, "Maybe you'll get away with it, but I doubt it. The forged signatures prove knowledge and intent, your boyfriend's prints are all over the house and the weapon. Even if you do squeeze out of the murder, they've got you on extortion, conspiracy, forgery, fraud, and grand theft. Why not talk about it? Maybe you can make a mint with your life story."

She turned to look at me. The beautiful face, and the model's body.

"I was going out of my gourd in that house, you hear? He was so fucking dull! Mooning over me. Always wantin' to stay *home*, for God's sake. Those nerd friends of his. That dead town! I had to get *out* of there! Fly! Then Eddie showed up."

"That was his real name after all? Eddie McBride?"

She ignored me. "Rode in on his damn old bike, and was ready! We was gonna fly, and I mean fly. Then it hit me how damn much he looked like Alan, and we got the idea. I mean, we had to have cash to go on, right? They owed me!"

"How'd you get the letter?"

"Found it on Alan after we whacked him. Don't know what the hell he was gonna do with it, maybe make his old man stop doin' bad things, the jerk, but we knew what to do. We'd have squeezed a bundle out of Ian!" She thrashed on the bare bed like a chained cat. "It was so *easy*, until that shitty brother of mine moved in! I'm glad he's dead, the son-of-a-bitch!"

It was still impossible to reconcile her face and body with her voice and gutter manner. We have strange prejudices, preconceptions.

"You knew Murdoch was after you before you left Chatham."

"We didn't know nothin' before he grabbed us in New York!"

I shook my head. "You doodled on a telephone pad: FREAK, Freak, freak. You at least talked to Jasper on the phone."

She laughed. "Shit, that wasn't Jasper. That was that freak husband of mine. He wanted to *touch* me every damned minute. He was so damned *nice* all the time. The freak!" She stopped laughing, looked at me. "I'm glad they're all dead. I had it. A bike and the whole country. A motorcycle all my fucking own, you hear! Mine!"

Her beautiful face was almost crying as I walked out. In the hospital corridor I found Steve Norris, Leah Aherne, and Max Aherne waiting for me. Norris was holding Leah's hand.

"I guess she likes old men." Norris grinned.

"I'm old," I said.

Leah said, "He needs me, Dan, you don't. He needs to feel it's not all over. You've made your own way to go on. You have your work."

"I'm going on my own, Dan," Norris said. "A security agency. My wife won't try."

I didn't think he'd do it. For all his talk of freedom, he'd end up working again for Max Aherne, settle for a new woman.

"If Ian won't pay you, Fortune, the company will. I'm running it again," Max Aherne said. He was pleased with events, with himself. The past was the past. "Norris says you have the letter all the fuss was about. Ian's resigned from active management, the deal won't happen. I wonder if the police have to see the letter after all? I mean, it seems a shame to perhaps ruin the company, hurt so many innocent people."

"Without the letter there's no case against Campbell or that government man who took the bribe."

"They've lost the deal, isn't that enough? Who gains?"

"Sorry," I lied. "I already gave it to the New Jersey State Police and the sheriff in Flagstaff."

I left Chatham the same way I'd come, crossing the Passaic River twice within fifteen miles. A journey from comfort and beauty and security into pain and garbage and violence, from a clean little river to the flowing swamp at Newark.

Back in my office I called Lieutenant DeVasto down in Derry City and told him about Dog and Mrs. Schott and that ended it. Except for the letter. I sent the original to the New Jersey State Police, notarized copies to Flagstaff and New York for their files. Maybe I'm the freak.

Order now the spine-tingling mysteries you missed in stores.

"Nothing is more satisfying than a mystery concocted by one of the pros." —*L.A. Times*

Hugh Pentecost
Winner of the Mystery Writers of America Award

TIME OF TERROR $3.50 [ ]
The elegant calm of New York's plush Hotel Beaumont is shattered
when a heavily-armed madman plants bombs in the building and
holds two guests hostage. Manager Pierre Chambrun's only chance is
to outwit the ruthless killer at his own game.

BARGAIN WITH DEATH $3.50 [ ]
Pierre Chambrun, legendary manager of Hotel Beaumont has only
hours to find the answers to some lethal questions when a ruthless
killer turns the hotel into a deathtrap.

REMEMBER TO KILL ME $3.50 [ ]
Pierre Chambrun must cope with the shooting of a close friend, a
hostage situation and a gang of hoods terrorizing guests.

NIGHTMARE TIME $3.50 [ ]
After the disappearance of an Air Force major involved in the Star
Wars program, Chambrun must use some extraordinary measures to
decide whether the disappearance is an act of treason or the hotel is
harboring a killer with diplomatic immunity.

Total Amount	$	_____
Plus 75¢ Postage		.75
Payment Enclosed	$	_____

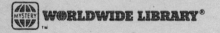 **WORLDWIDE LIBRARY**®